SCENE OF THE CRIME

He fumbled in the dark for a lantern. When he got it lit, he inspected the room—as large a bedroom as Stillman had ever seen, with a four-door armoire, a walk-in closet, and an oak four-poster bed. The bed had been stripped, but blood remained on the mattress—a great inky smudge that would never come out, no matter how long one of the hired girls scrubbed at it.

Stillman turned to one of the three windows and raised the lantern. The yellow light fell on the porch roof just below the window. The killer, hearing the hired girl, had gone out the window, onto the roof, and jumped from the roof to the ground.

"Crafty son of a bitch," Stillman carped aloud, staring at the light on the porch roof. Nimble one, too, he thought, to have jumped that far without breaking an ankle or leg.

Stillman stood staring out the window for a long time, his mind working over the possibilities, all the faces he'd seen, all the people he'd come to know, realizing that one of them was a killer.

Knowing he'd strike again . . .

ONCE
A
LAWMAN

PETER BRANDVOLD

BERKLEY BOOKS, NEW YORK

This is a work of fiction. Names, characters, places, and incidents are either the product of the author's imagination or are used fictitiously, and any resemblance to actual persons, living or dead, business establishments, events, or locales is entirely coincidental.

ONCE A LAWMAN

A Berkley Book / published by arrangement with
the author

PRINTING HISTORY
Berkley edition / November 2000

The Penguin Putnam Inc. World Wide Web site address is
http://www.penguinputnam.com

ISBN: 0-425-17773-4

BERKLEY®
Berkley Books are published by The Berkley Publishing Group,
a division of Penguin Putnam Inc.,
375 Hudson Street, New York, New York 10014.
BERKLEY and the "B" design
are trademarks belonging to Penguin Putnam Inc.

PRINTED IN THE UNITED STATES OF AMERICA

10 9 8 7 6 5 4

This book is for
Larry, Ellen, and Matt Brandvold
of Souris, North Dakota;
for my grandmother,
Alta Brandvold of Bottineau;
and in memory of my grandfather,
Olaf Brandvold,
who left us in 1999.

Thanks to all for their help and encouragement.

If thou wert the wolf, thy greediness
Would afflict thee, and oft thou
Shouldst hazard thy life for thy dinner.
　　　　　　　　—Shakespeare, *Timon of Athens*

1

IT WAS A grand night for a killing, he thought.

He crouched in the alley behind First Street in Clantick, Montana Territory, and lifted the collar of his tattered wool coat against the autumn chill.

A cool October wind shepherded leaves between trash heaps, privies, and stacks of split stove wood. A swollen lavender moon hung low over the buttes along the river, silhouetting the cottonwoods, box elders, and creaking aspens. The air smelled like frost-burned leaves and mown hay and wood smoke. Somewhere across town a dog howled, barely audible above the wind-muffled noise of a piano clattering in a side-street saloon.

The killer heard something else.

He turned to look between the buildings toward First Street. A horse-drawn surrey appeared there, carrying a man and a woman, both sitting very erect and stiff. The woman was driving. A man sat beside her. He was a medium-tall man in a business suit and a bowler hat, a newspaper clamped under his arm. Probably a horse buyer from Chicago or a whiskey drummer from Denver. It didn't matter. It wasn't the man the killer was interested in.

As the surrey passed on the street, the wind gusted, and the man reached up to secure the hat on his head. The woman's dress blew about her legs. They were pretty, almond-colored legs, the killer knew. He'd seen them through the window where the woman lived and worked.

As the surrey faded into the darkness down the street, the killer turned his head to look east down the alley. Just as he'd expected, the surrey reappeared there, at the end of the alley. It turned off First Street and was rolling down the side road.

The killer grinned, wiped a stream of chaw from his mouth with his wrist, and walked down the alley.

When he came to Second Avenue, he stood in the shadows of an overhang, between a gunsmith shop and a bakery, and watched the surrey disappear down the street on his left. There was only one saloon here, directly across the street from him, and it was quiet tonight, a weeknight. It wasn't a payday, either, so most of the cowboys were out on the line or snoring away in their bunkhouses. Only two horses stood at the hitchrack before the saloon, and the yellow light from the gas lamps did not spread far from the establishment's dirty windows.

The killer was alone out here and virtually invisible.

Yes, it was a good night for a killing.

He turned and followed the surrey. It was cloaked by the darkness now, and the wind covered the clomp of the horse's hooves. It didn't matter. The killer was in no hurry. He knew where the man and the woman were going, and he had all night.

When the killer came to the end of the block, he'd come to the end of the town. The road stretched beyond to the river coursing through the sage and yucca-covered buttes and several groves of trees in which drifters and dodgers often camped. There didn't appear to be anyone out there tonight, however. No campfires flickered in the darkness.

The killer breathed deeply of the fall wind, blinking as a leaf blew against his face, and followed the road for half a mile. He turned left down a two-track wagon trail, curving through a cow pasture. After about a hundred yards he came to a barn hulking up in the darkness, its open loft doors creaking in the wind. The trail curved around the barn and off to a log cabin sitting back in the trees by the river. The cabin was about a hundred yards away, and the killer could not see it in the darkness, but he knew that once the woman had stabled the horse and surrey in the shed, the cabin windows would be lit.

The cabin had been built by a trapper working the Milk and its tributaries. Then a drifter and con artist named Hank Stubb had moved in and turned the loft into a brothel, where he'd put a couple half-breed Indian girls to work, entertaining the men of fledgling Clantick and the cowboys who passed on the trail. Stubb had been in business two years when one of his girls hacked him to death with a scythe. The place lay abandoned until a year ago, when the current occupant moved in, fixed the place up, and planted shrubs and flowers in the yard.

The killer made his way to the barn and sat with his back to an outside wall, where he could watch the cabin. Soon a soft yellow light permeated the darkness, marking the cabin's windows. The killer stared at the light. He'd wait here for the gentleman to leave the woman—most of them walked the half-mile back to town, rather than have the lady drive them in the surrey. Then, when the woman was alone, he'd pay her a visit.

Thinking of this, the killer touched the knife and scabbard on his belt. Then he sank back against the barn wall, produced his sack of tobacco and papers, and began forging a cigarette.

With the wind blowing as hard as it was, creaking the barn behind him, it took him several attempts, facing the barn and hunkering over the flame, to light the cigarette. When he finally had it lit, he turned back around and got comfortable with his back to the barn wall, outstretched legs crossed at the ankles.

He'd smoked the quirley, rubbed it out on the ground, and was sitting there, growing impatient—

the lady's customers did not normally linger this long—when he heard something in the grass. Before he could turn to look, a figure appeared on his left, as though materializing from the darkness itself. It was the gentleman. He'd left the trail, cutting across the pasture toward town. Before the killer could move his legs, the man tripped over them, gave a curse, and fell headlong into the tall grass, cursing.

The man turned to the killer, who could not see his face but could tell from the harsh, angry breaths and faint groans what kind of expression the man had formed. "What . . . what the hell . . . ?"

"Watch where you're goin', ya clumsy oaf," the killer snarled.

The man pushed himself to his feet and retrieved his bowler. Turning to the killer, he said, "Who are you and what"—he bent to brush his trousers—"what the hell are you doing out here in the middle of the damn . . . ?"

His voice trailed off as the killer got to his feet and approached him, staring at him savagely. "That's okay," the man backpedaled. "It—it was my fault. I should watch where I'm going."

He turned to hurry away. The killer grabbed his shoulder and spun him around. His voice was urgent now, frightened. Pleading. "No, look . . . I said it was my fault—"

The killer pulled the knife out of its scabbard. Starlight danced on the blade.

"Wait, now . . . what . . . what are you doing?" the

man said, his voice brittle with fear as his eyes discovered the knife. He was trying to move away, but the killer kept his vicelike hand clamped on the man's shoulder.

"I'm going to kill you," the killer said in a voice chill with certainty.

Before the man could say anything else, the killer plunged the knife into his midsection. He gave a startled grunt, bending forward at the waist. The killer removed his left hand from his shoulder, and the man took two steps backward, crouched over the wound in his belly. The air left his lungs in one long wheeze. He stumbled, fell on his back, wheezing and groaning, legs shaking involuntarily.

The killer stood over the man, looking into the shocked expression on the man's face. Then he knelt and grabbed the knife to finish the man, who lifted his head to say in a whisper, "Why?"

"You'll never know," the killer said with a wry, self-satisfied chuckle. He removed the knife from the man's abdomen and slashed it across his throat, finishing him.

He wiped the knife blade in the grass and stood. He returned the knife to the sheath on his belt, turned, and headed for the cabin, its pale lights still aglow in the darkness. Fists in his coat pockets, chaw under his lip, he strolled as though he were going to see the woman on business—just another Clantick citizen with the nighttime itch.

He walked boldly up to a window and peered in.

The woman was there, smoking a thin cheroot while she poured steaming water into a copper tub. A green lamp shed buttery light from a shelf above the tub where catalogs and tattered dime books and newspapers were stacked. The killer could tell by the set of the woman's full, mulatto mouth that she was humming a little tune to herself, happy now that the night was over and that she'd filled her quota of customers for the day. Maybe the gentleman had given her a little extra with which to buy something pretty for herself or to take a day off and go on a picnic.

She'd no doubt enjoy a picnic, a chance to get away by herself and take a ride in the mountains or along the river, pick some flowers to replace the dead ones in the wicker basket by the door.

The killer stared through the small, sashed window and smiled with his cold eyes, feeling the bite of old anger crawl up from his bowels.

Yeah, she'd like that, wouldn't she?

When the woman had finished filling the tub, she took a long drag off the cheroot, set the cheroot in an ashtray on a shelf with the lamp and the books, and unbuttoned her sheer, pink wrapper. The killer was not surprised to see that she wore nothing beneath the wrapper, nor was he surprised at the woman's beauty: the full breasts and hips, slender arms and thighs, smooth belly, flawless skin the color of varnished oak, with a smattering of black freckles in her cleavage.

No, he wasn't surprised. He'd been here before, standing outside a window as she lay on her back, long shapely legs wrapped around some groaning cowpoke's thrusting hips.

Her full breasts swayed now as she leaned to hang the wrapper on a wall peg. Turning and removing the pins from her hair, loosening the bun at her neck so the black, curly mass spiraled about her shoulders, she poked a foot in the tub, gave her head a shake to distribute the hair evenly about her shoulders, neck, and back, and stepped into the tub. Smiling thinly at the water's comforting heat, she put both hands on the sides of the tub and gently lowered herself into the tendrils of steam rising from the water and pasting her hair against her skin.

Her smile widening, she sighed and lay back against the tub. She retrieved the cheroot from the ashtray on the shelf and stuck it between her lips, taking a long, luxurious drag. Exhaling a thin plume of smoke, she smiled again and sank lower in the tub. She sat that way, eyes closed, lips etched in a smile, for several minutes. Then she returned the cheroot to the ashtray, stood, and began sponging her arms and neck and shoulders, her breasts and belly and legs. She lifted each foot, balancing with one hand on the side of the tub, to give each a doting scrub.

The killer stared at her soapy, swaying breasts, at the expanding and contracting muscles in her belly, at the wet hair brushing her forehead. He swallowed.

When the woman had sat down in the tub again and returned the cheroot to her lips, the killer turned and moved to the door, his movements stiff with lust and hate.

When he came to the door, he turned the knob. The woman had forgotten to lock it, as she had many times. She rarely had trouble here; she entertained only one customer at a time, and pleased him well. The door opened and fell back against the wall.

The woman turned to the killer with surprise, covering her breasts with her left arm. "Hey!" she yelled. "I'm closed!" Her voice was husky with anger.

The killer said nothing. He stood in the open doorway and stared at her with cunning humor.

"I said get out of here!" the woman shouted. Her face was red with anger. The cheroot smoldered in the hand clutching her breasts.

The killer just stood there. The woman looked him up and down. A light of recognition shone in her eyes. Her eyes widened and her mouth opened. Her expression turned amused, and she nearly laughed. She brought her hand to her mouth, leaving her breasts exposed. "Why you're . . . you're . . ."

"That's right," the killer said.

"Where's your—?"

"At home."

The woman gave one loud laugh. Then her eyes went serious again, and there was a hesitating look on her face. "Why . . . ?"

Something dawned on her, and her eyes flickered cold fear. Suddenly she was on her feet, splashing water from the tub. Then she was running for the back door, naked and half-slipping, clawing at the door, muttering and stammering with tongue-tied fright. After several tries, she got the door open, threw it wide, and plunged into the night.

Not having anticipated such a reaction—he hadn't expected her to remember him, nor had he expected her to be able to bolt so quickly from the tub—the killer was only halfway across the room when the woman had dashed out the cabin door.

He lunged for it now and peered into the night. Something flickered in the darkness straight out from the cabin, and he ran toward it.

He soon saw the woman, running and stumbling on her bare feet. She was whimpering and yelling for help, but the wind covered her voice. There was a chance, however, that she would make it to the river where some grubliner might be camped in the weeds, without a fire.

The killer felt a pang of fear, and his anger grew. He ran, boots pounding, after the yelling woman who was little more than a pale flicker in the darkness before him.

He ran past the buggy shed in which the horse whinnied an answer to the woman's screams, and down the bank lined with willows. Then he stopped suddenly when he saw the woman on the ground before him.

She'd tripped in a gully and was struggling to her feet. She was having a hard time because she'd injured an ankle. When she saw him, she screamed. This time the scream carried loudly. The killer threw himself atop her and covered her mouth with his hands. She struggled, fought his hand a few inches away from her mouth, and screamed again, but he managed to clamp his hand back on her mouth, clipping the scream. With his powerful left fist, he hit her, hard, on the side of the head.

He grabbed her arms and pinned her to the ground. Semiconscious, her head lolled from side to side. She gave halfhearted kicks. Against the killer's overwhelming power, they were little more than the flailing of a dying fish.

Regaining control, the killer smiled again and straddled the naked woman. Glancing around to make sure no one had heard the woman's pleas and come running, he grabbed his knife from his scabbard and held it before her face. The sight of the blade paralyzed her. She went limp in the killer's arms.

In a small voice, pleading for her life, she said, "I'm . . . sorry . . ."

The killer grinned. "Yes, you are," he hissed.

Then he flourished his knife and cut her throat.

2

THE WIDOW BJORNSON pulled her red-wheeled buggy off the trail north of Clantick and heaved back on the reins, yelling to the beefy sorrel in harness, "Woah now, Ole! Woooooah! . . . That's it."

The widow tied the reins to the brake handle and turned to speak to her nieces. But the two girls—blond, blue-eyed, big-boned, and decked out in colorfully embroidered dresses and white cotton bonnets—had already jumped down from the buggy and were running down the gentle, brushy grade to the river.

A month ago they'd arrived from Norway to help the widow in her sewing business, which had grown by leaps and bounds in the past year. They'd seen little of the frontier so far but the dim inside of a tidy clapboard house and sewing room, with the monotonous ticks of the widow's numerous clocks she'd shipped from the Old World. So they were excited to spend the morning out of doors.

The widow aimed her blunt nose and cold gray eyes down the grade, where the girls were running and laughing, holding hands and pushing playfully away from each other. As a First Street loafer had once remarked, the widow had been stricken with buzzardlike features and the physique of a sturdy well house. Her voice was high and lilting, with the barking quality of quarreling crows.

"Slow down now, girls," she yelled. "You break your ankles and I haf to ship you back to Norvay!"

The big woman arranged her dull gray dress and petticoats with one hand as she carefully lowered herself from the buggy, grunting and working her nearly toothless mouth with the effort and reprimanding the horse to stand still. When she had her feet solidly planted on hard ground, she ambled to the back of the buggy and retrieved a spade with a hickory handle and a bushel-sized wicker basket.

The spade in one hand, basket in the other, she started down the slope toward the river, which flowed beyond the trees and shrubs lining the bank. Twice she nearly slipped in the grass, her heavy black shoes offering little purchase. She cursed in Norwegian and wheezed as she plunged the spade down for support.

"Girlsss," she piped, "you could stay and help your aunty here now!"

By the time she'd made it to the bottom of the grade, the girls had disappeared, but she could hear them giggling and chattering in Norwegian, about thirty yards away. A splash told the widow they'd thrown something in the water.

Canada geese were quarreling on the opposite bank, every day their flocks growing larger and larger as their southern migration loomed. Looking up at the pearly-pink morning sky, not a cloud in sight, the widow saw a flock angling southwestward, toward the field stubble the sun had recently discovered beyond Clantick.

"Just a couple o' blackbirds, you sound," the widow screeched at the girls. "Speak English!"

The widow rested a moment on the spade handle, catching her breath and feeling sweat trickle under the many layers of cotton she always wore—it was an unusually warm morning for this late in the year. There was nary a hint of autumn chill, and the dew hadn't even frozen in the grass last night. The weather changed so suddenly out here, where the mountain chinooks often blew.

Tightening her scarf and sighing with resolve, the widow began walking downstream, her shoes crackling in the damp grass and the dew soaking her skirts. From beneath the fluttering scarf, she eyed the shrubs and bushes that grew thick between her and the water, scrutinizing each for size and health. She intended to dig a half dozen chokecherry bushes and replant them in her yard, for both the berries and for a hedge, which would keep that hooligan Hazel Mulroney, the Irish druggist's wife who lived next door to Mrs. Bjornson, from sneaking peeks at the widow's wash.

"Here . . . this looks good," the widow said to herself, halting near a cluster of what appeared to be two-year-old chokecherry shrubs. Their leaves had turned red and had been burned and curled by frost, but their slender, iron-colored trunks appeared firm and healthy. They'd transplant nicely and grow like weeds come spring. In a few years that Irish would have to climb a ladder to see over their berry-laden tops!

The widow set down the basket, took the spade in both hands, set the blade point on the ground about a foot away from one of the shrubs, and used one of her heavy black shoes to plunge it into the sod, giving a deep grunt and a sigh. As she labored she imagined her broad, work-toughened hands moving automatically over a clump of the small, plum-colored berries as she picked them—right in her own yard! She brightened, remembering her late husband Per, who had died only seven months after they'd arrived on the frontier and who had loved the sweetened juice of the berries over a heaping bowl of ice cream.

The widow had about four spadefuls of sod scooped out of the ground when she suddenly realized she could hear only the river gurgling over a beaver dam, the buzz of blackflies, and the screech of blackbirds in a nearby cottonwood copse.

Where were the girls?

Stricken with the image of one of her nieces floating facedown in the river, the widow opened her mouth to yell. Before she'd formed the first word, the silence gave way to a scream. It was a drum-throbbing, high-pitched scream only a girl can produce—a girl in great duress, suddenly shocked and horrified. Startled birds churned from the trees. A moment later, another scream joined the first.

"Borgy! Hilda!" the widow yelled, dropping the spade and moving as quickly toward the screams as her heavy legs would allow.

The girls appeared, running out of the bushes, their faces twisted in terror, blue eyes wide with fear.

"Aunty, Aunty!" Borgy screamed in Norwegian.

"What is it?" the widow replied in her native tongue, voice tinged with anger as well as concern. Seeing that both girls were safe, she thought they'd probably only stumbled upon a dead fish. They'd nearly given her a stroke over a carp!

Both girls ran to her and got behind her, as if using her to shield them from whatever horror they'd come upon in the shrubs. Each was crying and yanking on one of the widow's hands.

"What is it, silly children?" the widow asked again in Norwegian. "What did you see?"

Borgy dropped to the ground, pulling at weeds and crying. Hilda grabbed the widow's hand and stomped her feet. "There's a lady," she cried. "There's a lady . . . in the trees . . . !"

The widow frowned, skeptical. "What's this you say?"

"There's a dead lady in the trees!"

The widow repeated the words to herself, moving her lips, then regarded the girls seriously, brows furrowed. Hilda sat down next to her sister and hugged her knees, crying uncontrollably, terror etched in her round, pink face.

"You wait here," the widow said in English.

Turning, she headed for the place in the bushes where the girls had first appeared. It took her a good five minutes to make her way through the brambles, nearly tripping several times and having to stop to work her skirts free of the hawthorns. When she'd finally made it to the river, where yellow foam washed against the bank and the rotten smell of the river rose to her nose, she froze, her mouth opening in a silent gasp.

"Oh, my . . . oh, my," she intoned, pressing a hand to her heaving bosom. She swallowed to keep from vomiting and grabbed a branch to turn herself around. Heading back the way she'd come, she made it back to the girls in half the time it had taken her to reach the river.

"All right, girls, back to the buggy," she said with characteristic sternness and strained calm. "Back to the buggy now. Wait. Don't leave me! Here . . . help your aunty!" She held out her hands, and both girls checked their hasty retreat to turn, take the widow's arms, and half carry her up the grade to the buggy.

•   •   •

Fay Stillman sat at the kitchen table of the small frame house she and Ben had bought two months ago on French Street, and went over her students' composition themes with a pen. She paused occasionally to sip her coffee and glance at the clock. She'd given her students the morning off, as there had been a death in Gerald Pepin's prominent family, but she had told them she'd see them all in the one-room schoolhouse promptly at noon.

Like the house, teaching was something new in Fay's life. She'd taken the job when the previous teacher married a rancher from Chinook, and the city council, unable to find any other qualified applicants, asked Fay if she'd give it a shot. While Fay was mostly self-taught, she'd been blessed with a keen, curious mind and a love for books and learning. What's more, she was bilingual, and could teach French as well as English. Since boredom was a fact of life in remote Clantick, Montana Territory, and since Fay had begun to fear her unchallenged mind would calcify, she'd jumped at the offer.

Now she scribbled a delighted, "Very nice evocation" on Mattie Lawrence's two-paragraph theme, set her pen in the red ink bottle before her, and picked up her coffee cup. Hearing Ben hammering on the old buggy house to which he was adding a chicken coop in the backyard, she smiled. She found her husband's fascination for chickens, which he had raised as a boy in Pennsylvania and then again while recovering from a back wound in Great Falls, just another endearing aspect of the big, rugged man's character. Fay loved her husband more than life itself, and while life here in Clantick could be a bore at times, she did not begrudge his leaving the Pinkerton Agency in Denver to come here and accept the job as Hill County Sheriff.

Ben Stillman was first and foremost a frontier lawman. Not even the drunk whore who'd shot him in Virginia City, forcing him to retire his marshal's badge, could take that away from him. Fay couldn't, nor did she want to. She herself could never be happy unless he was happy. And here in Clantick, on Montana's remote Hi-Line, only forty miles from Canada, Fay was happy indeed.

Thoughtfully, she sipped her coffee, which had cooled. As she set the cup down and stood to retrieve the pot from the range, she saw something move out the living room window and heard the clomp of galloping hooves and the rattle and leathery squeak of a fast-moving buggy.

Fay turned to give the window her full attention. Sweeping her rich black hair from her eyes, she saw the buggy pull to a stop before the house. In the buggy sat the Widow Bjornson and her two nieces, who'd recently moved to Clantick to help the widow with her sewing business.

At first, Fay thought the widow had come to say she'd reconsidered Fay's invitation to enroll the girls in school. But Fay could tell by the horrified looks on the girls' faces and by the pinched, urgent expression on the widow's that that wasn't their business at all.

Fay got up and met the harried widow at the front door. "Mrs. Bjornson," Fay said with concern, "what—?"

"Yah, yah," the widow said, holding onto the porch rail for dear life. Her face was flushed, and her scarf had blown back on her head. "Where's your husband . . . where's the sher'ff?"

"Out back," Fay said. "Can—?" But before she could say anything else, the widow had turned and, in her shuffling gait, disappeared around the side of the house.

Stillman was tacking chicken wire to a post he'd planted in the ground. He'd tethered his bay horse nearby. Sweets was cropping grass near the old well pump when he lifted his head sharply and cocked an ear.

Stillman turned from his work. At first he thought the noise he and Sweets had heard was a bird of some kind. Then he heard "Sheriff" shrieked. His hammer in his hand and two steel staples in his mouth, he watched the Widow Bjornson come around the house and shuffle toward him, heavy skirts whipping about her enormous hips.

Stillman felt himself clench at the sight of the old woman, never one to brighten your day. With some effort, Stillman fashioned a smile, plucking the staples from his lips. The widow was not given to unannounced social calls. He figured she was here to complain again about her neighbors.

Attempting to disarm the woman with charm, he said heartily, "Mrs. Bjornson, to what do I owe—?"

"Mr. Stillman, I thought they made you the law around here," the widow scolded, coming to a stop so close to Stillman that he could smell her vinegar breath, see the deep wrinkles etched in her face.

Stillman studied the woman, puzzled. "The city council gave me the job last summer, ma'am. You know that."

"Yes, they made you sheriff. Then why are you not out sheriffing?"

Stillman shrugged, looking guiltily down at the wire he'd been stringing. "Well, it's been pretty quiet around here lately, and I thought I'd take a few hours this morning to get my chicken house ready for next spring. A man can't work outside much in the winter around here, and—"

"Yes, you are working on your chickens," the widow said, as though scolding a disobedient child. "And where is the black man, your dep-u-ty?"

Stillman sighed, involuntarily reverting to his boyhood self, when his grandmother, whose resemblance to the Widow Bjornson was frightening, would scold him for not splitting the wood just right or for sneaking out of his room at night to roll cigarettes behind the barn. "I . . . I gave him the morning off. He worked late last night, and I thought if

anyone had any trouble this morning, well . . . they'd
know where to find me." His face warmed with guilt
and irritation.

"Yes, you are not doing your job," the widow
summarized. "And that is why, when I take my
nieces down to the river this morning to dig trees,
we find a dead woman in the bushes. In the bushes!
Dead!"

"What?"

"A dead woman in the bushes!" the widow cried,
lifting her arms. *"Oof-ta!* There is a nude woman
lying dead in the bushes along the river. And do you
know who found this dead, nude woman?"

"Whereabouts along the—?"

"My nieces!"

"Whereabouts along the river, Mrs. Bjornson?"

"Behind that mulatto's house."

"Is it the mulatto?"

"I don't know if it's de mulatto. I didn't linger.
That's your job!"

"Ah . . . heck," Stillman muttered, turning away
from the old woman to consider the information.
Since he and his deputy, Leon McMannigle, had
come to town and gotten the place relatively civilized, the town and county had been about as quiet
as you could expect this far north and west. There'd
only been one murder in the past few months, and
that had been a Russian farmer killed by his wife
when she'd discovered him diddling her niece in
their barn loft.

The old woman continued her tirade. "Ah heck is right. When you get up in the morning to do an honest day's work, thinking the town is finally a safe place to raise your nieces from Norvay—"

"Yes, I'm very sorry about that, Mrs. Bjornson," Stillman said, taking the old woman by the arm and leading her back around the house. "I'm very sorry you and your nieces had to be assaulted by such a spectacle—on such a fine morning, too," he continued, drowning out the widow's continuing, ever-growing onslaught of invectives. "But I appreciate your letting me know. Leon and I will get right on it. We'll get the body hauled out of there and you can go back to your tree planting. There, that's it," he said as he helped her through the gate in the picket fence, then onto the buggy.

Stillman saw Fay standing beside the buggy, holding Borgy's hand in hers. The girls had stopped crying, but their faces were swollen and tear-streaked, their disheveled hair spilling out of their bonnets.

Helping the widow get seated beside the brake, Stillman turned to the nieces. "Borgy, Hilda, I'm awfully sorry—" But before he could finish, the widow flicked the reins against the sorrel's back and gave an angry yell, scaring the horse into an immediate, lurching canter. Suddenly Ben and Fay stood there alone, a buggy's width apart, blinking their eyes against the dust.

"What was that all about?" Fay asked him.

"Borgy and Hilda tried to tell me, but their English isn't very good. All I could decipher is that they found someone dead somewhere."

"Behind the mulatto woman's cabin," Stillman said, staring after the buggy, which turned the corner and headed south, toward the widow's prim house and yard.

"Who is it—did she say?"

"No," Stillman said, shaking his head. He turned to his lovely wife darkly. "Just said it was a naked woman."

"The . . . mulatto woman?" Fay asked, tentative.

Stillman shook his head. "She didn't know."

Fay mirrored her husband's troubled frown. "Heaven help us."

3

HEAVEN HELP US, was right, Stillman thought as he shrugged into the clean shirt Fay held out for him and buttoned it. A woman lay dead along the river. A naked woman. He didn't know why that made a difference, but it did.

He hoped it was only a drowning, but something told him it wasn't. Something told him that Clantick wasn't quite as quiet as it had appeared in recent months. This troubled him. Stillman took pride in making the citizens of Hill County feel protected as they went about their lives on the frontier. He felt personally responsible for the safety of everyone in his jurisdiction, and he took any indication of trouble personally.

Hearing the widow's admonishment over and over in his head—"Then why are you not out sheriffing?"—he wrapped his .44 and cartridge belt around his waist and donned his ten-gallon Stetson. He kissed Fay on his way to the door. Fay grabbed his arm, clamped his big, weathered face in her hands, and stared into his eyes.

"You're not a clairvoyant," she said, reprimandingly. "You can't always know when there's going to be trouble."

"I know," he said without heat.

"Besides, she probably drowned."

"Probably."

Fay sighed, knowing her efforts were futile. Ben wanted to be father of the world, keep everyone from harm in spite of the fact that things just didn't work that way. She kissed him on the lips, hard.

"I'll see you later, Mr. Stillman," she said, giving her husband an encouraging smile. Sometimes that was all she could do.

"See you later, Mrs. Stillman," he said, returning the smile.

In the buggy shed he saddled his horse, remembering the bay needed a new right rear shoe. Cursing himself for not getting the shoe replaced yesterday— there's another thing he should have done instead of tending his chicken house—he led the horse out of the shed, around the house, and down the street.

Taking a shortcut through an alley and across a vacant lot, he entered Carney's blacksmith shop, which sat two blocks down from the jailhouse on First Street, five minutes later. The shop's wide doors were pushed back, revealing the forge glowing hotly. Before the forge worked the smithy, Jeff Carney, who was shaping a landside with a hammer.

It never ceased to amaze Stillman how the man could run a blacksmith shop—shoeing horses, welding, and shaping plowshares—from a wheelchair. He had custommade the chair himself, with larger wheels than normal, and a system of pulleys that raised and lowered the seat.

"Mornin', Jeff," Stillman called through the doors. "Can you replace Sweets's right rear shoe sometime this morning?"

Jeff Carney was a big, broad-shouldered man with the hands and forearms of a giant and the withered, useless legs of a cripple. Stillman hadn't asked what malaise had stricken the man, and Carney hadn't offered the information.

He turned his chair to Stillman with a flick of his right arm. "Well, I'm kind of backed up here, Ben," the man said, nodding to the two buggies and the hay rake parked before the open doors.

"I see that, but we might have a killer on the loose, and I'd like to have my horse handy if I need him," Stillman said.

"Killer?" Carney said, blinking away the coal soot from his eyelashes.

"Apparently there's a dead woman down by the river. I have to find Leon and have a look. Will you do it?"

Carney nodded, set his hammer on the anvil, and wheeled toward Sweets. "Get right on it," he said with gravity.

"Thanks, Jeff," Stillman said, walking off.

"Whatever I can do to help, Ben."

Stillman walked across the street, past Hall's Mercantile and a bakery, and turned down the side street, where all three of the town's brothels sat, side by side. Stillman went into the one whose shingle read simply, Rooms by the Hour.

All the rooms downstairs were vacant, so Stillman went up the steep, narrow staircase to the second floor, where four rooms opened off a dark hall.

"Leon?" he called.

No answer.

"Leon?"

Someone moved in one of the rooms. The floor creaked, and a door opened. A girl with a china doll's face stood there in a wrapper, yawning. "He's in here," she said, hooking her thumb over her shoulder.

Stillman stepped past her and cast his gaze at the bed, which nearly filled the tiny room. A look of surprise entered his eyes, and his eyebrows went up involuntarily. Two young women—a brunette and a blonde—lay curled up on either side of Stillman's black deputy, Leon McMannigle, a thin sheet drawn up to their waists. Leon lay faceup, eyes closed, a thin smile etched on his lips.

Stillman looked at the girl standing by the door, a question in his eyes.

She shrugged. "We were slow last night, and you know how we all favor Leon." Her eyes went smoky as she looked at the deputy. "That man is . . . all man," she said, a note of awe in her voice.

Stillman gave his head a shake. Then he walked to the bed and clapped his hands together twice loudly and piped, "Come on, lover! Up and at 'em! We got work to do!"

McMannigle's eyes snapped open. Jerking the blonde onto her back, Leon flung his right arm toward the holstered revolver hanging on the front bedpost to his left.

"Hold it! Hold it, Leon! It's Ben."

The black man froze, his right hand on the gun's grips. He turned his head, eyes still bright with surprise, to Stillman. Holding up his hands placatingly, Stillman said, "Easy." He should have known better than to startle the man out of sleep that way. McMannigle had fought Apaches in Arizona, and any sudden noise while he drowsed brought Nana and his compadres back in earnest.

McMannigle relaxed and gave a ragged sigh. "Whew—I thought you was trouble, Ben."

"Sorry," Stillman said, retrieving the man's long johns from the mess of clothes strewn about the floor. "I guess in a way I am." He tossed the long johns on the bed. "I'll wait downstairs."

He'd waited only five minutes when Leon appeared, tucking his shirt in his pants, black, flat-brimmed hat on his head, and Remington revolver tied low on his lean hip. "What's happened?" he asked.

Stillman sent a boy for Doc Evans and his hearse

and told his deputy everything he knew on their way to the river.

"Whereabouts she at?" Leon asked as they cut between stores and headed north of town, through yards and pastures.

"Behind the mulatto's place, I guess."

They descended the grade behind the cabin, the dewy morning grass dampening their boots and trouser cuffs. Most of the dew had dried, however, and the sun was heating up, bringing out the sweat on Stillman's neck. It was going to be a warm October day. Stillman had intended to spend the morning on his chicken coop and the afternoon going over the court docket the county judge had updated. Now those plans had changed. He was going to be informing someone of a death in their family and possibly hunting a killer.

"Why don't you look upstream and I'll look down?" Stillman said when they'd come to the trees along the river.

He looked at Leon, gazing downstream with interest. Stillman glanced that way and did a double take. A dog was ambling out of the brush along the river. The small, stiff-eared mongrel saw Stillman and McMannigle, turned, and headed in the opposite direction, casting a sheepish look behind.

Stillman and Leon regarded each other knowingly and headed downstream. When they came to where the dog had left the brush, they headed into the shrubs, parting branches with their hands.

"Here she is," Stillman said regretfully, finding the body on the muddy bank, water lapping at her naked legs.

The woman lay on her side, one arm thrown over her face as though to block the light, heavy black hair fanned out in the mud and leaves and stringy grass. Stillman jerked his trousers up his thighs and squatted on his haunches with a sigh. He regarded the body for a moment, Leon hovering over him, hands on his thighs. Stillman reached out, grabbed the woman's stiff arm, and pulled her onto her back.

Stillman winced. The gash in the woman's neck was long and deep, exposing dried blood, gristle, and bone. Her skin was almond, with a blue cast. The lips were swollen.

"Well, it's her . . . and she sure as hell didn't drown," Stillman said.

McMannigle squatted next to Stillman. "Cadena Martin."

Stillman looked at him. "That her name? I guess I didn't even know. Just knew her as the mulatto."

"That's how most people knew her."

"She run her place all by herself?"

Leon nodded. He was staring at the body sadly. "Yeah, she ran it all by herself. She was a little different from the other girls. Preferred to be off by herself. The other girls didn't care for her much. Said she was uppity. I'd go by and talk to her some. She just preferred working alone, that's all."

Stillman regarded his deputy with interest. The

black man, because of his color, which set him apart from the "respectable" whites of the town, seemed to know a whole different side of Clantick and Hill County than the one Stillman knew. While Stillman knew the bankers and storekeepers on First Street, Leon preferred the company of the drifters and the dodgers and the pleasure girls, the gypsies and the transient Indian families that often camped by the river. He'd even known this Cadena Martin, whose presence Stillman had been aware of, but only vaguely. He'd never taken an interest. To him she'd been just another looney pleasure girl plying her trade in her shack down by the river.

"I told her she shouldn't work alone down here," Leon mumbled, as if to himself.

"You have any idea who might have killed her?" Stillman asked.

Leon shrugged and shook his head. "It could've been anybody, Ben." He sighed. "Anybody."

"Did you see her yesterday?"

Leon ran his hands down his bristly cheeks, bringing his fingers and thumb together at his chin. A light flickered in his muddy eyes. "Yeah . . . I seen her walk by the Drovers Saloon last night. I was in there tryin' to dull the horns on a couple quarreling gamblers. I seen her pass by the window. I bet she was heading for the train station." He looked at Stillman significantly. "She often went over to the train station at night. She liked the traveling drummers and soldiers and such 'cause they weren't around long, and their wives wouldn't come lookin' for her." He gave a meager smile.

"I reckon we better check out the train station, then," Stillman said, grunting as he straightened his legs. "And the hotels."

A wagon rattled in the distance. Stillman heard Doc Evans cajoling his horse. The sounds grew louder, and Stillman turned to see a flicker of movement through the trees.

He pushed through the shrubs and stepped in front of the black horse pulling a high-sided wagon painted black. Dressed in a tattered bowler, his thick red mustache and wavy red hair glistening in the golden morning light, Doc Evans sat in the driver's box. Seeing Ben, he pulled back on the reins, bringing the horse to a stop.

Evans looked more like a down-on-his-luck Eastern gambler than a doctor who moonlighted as an undertaker. Stillman thought the man's wry personality didn't fit his trade, either. But he also knew a tender heart lay beneath a layer or two of cynical sophistication.

"Morning," Stillman said.

"Is it?" the doctor said, setting the brake and climbing down with a grunt. "I haven't the marbles yet to notice. That kid you sent over pulled me out of a deep one."

"You stay up too late drinking alone," Stillman said. "Very bad habit. Take it from an expert."

"I was reading Virgil. You can drink alone as long

as you're reading the Greeks." He came up to Stillman, who could smell the booze on his breath. "What do you have?"

"Come on," Stillman said, and started into the brush.

"Hey!" someone yelled in the distance.

Stillman stopped and turned, looking around. A man in overalls and big floppy hat was standing behind the barn looming about a hundred yards northeast. At the edge of the barn's shadow, the man waved his arm, cupped his hands around his mouth, and yelled, "What are you doing over there? He's over here. *Bring the wagon!*"

4

STILLMAN, MCMANNIGLE, AND Doc Evans loaded the mulatto woman's body onto the wagon. Then Stillman and McMannigle sat on the end gate, legs hanging over the edge, as the doctor drove them over to where the farmer waited by his barn. Stillman had a very dark feeling about all this. The farmer had called for Evans's wagon, meaning he had to have a body. That made two. Two bodies in one morning, only about a hundred yards apart . . .

What the hell was happening to the town Stillman had worked so hard to quiet?

The doctor pulled the wagon up beside the farmer, who stood with his hands on his hips, gloves drooping out of a back pocket of his overalls, staring down at the bloody body of a suited man in the grass. Stillman and McMannigle stepped off the wagon and walked over for a closer look.

"Found him here t'is morning, ven I come out for

chores," the farmer said in a German accent thick enough to split with a wedge. Stillman knew his name was Gunther Tollefson. He farmed a few patches of corn but mostly hay, which he sold to the army garrisoned nearby at Fort Assiniboine.

"Did you hear anything last night, Gunther?" Stillman asked.

"Nein, not a t'ing. Dat wind, she was blowing pretty goot."

Stillman sighed and knelt next to the dead man. He was a well-dressed gent, probably in his early thirties, with muttonchops and a thick mustache. His suit and waistcoat were fine broadcloth, his shirt was silk, and the watch hanging out of his pocket was gold. The name Reginald Dawson had been engraved on the lid. Stillman clicked it open. A photograph of a young, dark-haired woman in an evening gown had been pasted inside.

"Stationery salesman," Doc Evans said. He was still sitting on the wagon, reins in his hands. He'd fallen uncharacteristically silent after seeing the dead woman. A strange reaction, Stillman thought, for such a wry, vocal man who dealt with death and sickness daily.

"What's that?" Stillman asked.

"He sells stationery to the mercantiles in town. Comes in once a month. I've played poker with him."

Stillman looked at the doctor with interest. "Did you play with him last night?"

"No. I didn't see him in any of the saloons before I packed it in."

"Why would someone kill him?" Leon said, voicing all their thoughts. "Didn't even take his watch, so it couldn't have been for money."

A thought occurring to him, Stillman lifted the stiffening body onto its side, felt around, and produced a light brown, calfskin wallet. Flipping it open, he counted fifty-two dollars. Business cards announced the man's name and address. He hailed from Bismarck, Dakota Territory, and worked for Munson & Tolliver: Sellers of Stationery and Fine Office Products Since 1865.

The information would allow Stillman to notify the man's relatives, and ship him home for burial, if they wanted. He figured they would. They could probably afford it. It was mostly the drifters whose families—if they had families—declined the offer to send the bodies home. They asked only for whatever money the deceased had had on his person—if there was any.

"*Ja,*" the farmer said, shaking his head darkly. "That's a nasty cut on his neck."

"I'll say," Stillman concurred. "And it's the same type of cut as the woman's. From the same knife, too, judging by the size of it."

He walked around, inspecting the ground. Finally, he pointed at something along the path leading to the cabin. "There's some footprints here, two sets, fairly fresh." He went back to the dead man and inspected the bottoms of his shoes. Walking back toward the cabin, he gazed at the ground, frowning, and then turned and came back toward the others.

"It's hard to tell, but I'd say he came from the cabin. I'd say whoever killed him was heading *toward* the cabin."

Leon looked at him. "You think whoever killed him might've just run into him on the trail?"

Stillman squinted his eyes and ran his tongue over his lips. Finally, he shrugged. "That or he could've been waiting for him to come out. Why don't you and the doc take these two over to Doc's barn, and lay 'em out."

"What are you going to do?" Leon asked as he and Stillman picked up the dead drummer and carried him to the wagon.

"I'm going to walk over to the cabin, see if I can come up with anything else."

They laid the man next to Cadena Martin in the wagon box, and Leon, wiping his bloody hands in the grass, said, "You think they were together last night?"

Stillman regarded the two people in the wagon box, both lying there with identical knife wounds laying their throats open. Cadena looked nightmarish and white, lying there nude, with her hazel eyes half open, head tilted slightly to one side, cheek snugged up against the shoulder of Reginald Dawson. Dawson just looked dead. Pale and sad and dead, all dressed up with nowhere to go but the grave.

"That's my guess," Stillman mused. "Maybe someone ran into him out here, figured he'd been visiting Miss Martin, and got jealous." He looked at Leon. "Did she have a steady fella?"

"None I knew about," Leon said. "Course that doesn't mean a man hadn't got fixated and wanted her all for himself. It happens sometimes to girls on the line."

"There was no one," Evans said from the wagon seat, his back to them. He'd spoken softly, elbows on his thighs, staring straight ahead, not looking at either Stillman or McMannigle.

"Say again, Doc?" Stillman said.

"As far as I knew, there was no one fixated on her. I think she would have told me."

Stillman glanced at Leon, who returned his weighty gaze.

Stillman had more questions for the doctor, who'd never made any bones about visiting pleasure girls, but decided they could wait until they were alone. They often got together in the afternoon for a beer and a hand or two of cards. Then the sheriff would ask him about his relationship with the mulatto woman.

"You two head on over to the barn," Stillman said. "I'll see you later."

When the wagon had pulled out, Stillman turned to the farmer, who was still standing where he'd been since they'd first pulled up. "Sorry about the trouble," he said to the man, touching Tollefson's shoulder and turning away.

"You're t' one with da trouble, Sheriff," Tollefson grunted, as Stillman started toward the cabin.

"You can say that again."

The front door of the cabin was standing open. Stillman walked inside slowly, feeling strange in light of what had happened. He'd always felt a little haunted when dealing with the personal effects of dead people.

A couple of lanterns were still lit, and a tub, half-full of water, sat in the middle of the main room, a kitchen with a range, some makeshift cupboards, a small table with wildflowers in a vase, and two chairs. The suds in the bathwater had dispersed. Dipping his hand, Stillman found the water had cooled. Looking up, he saw a thin cheroot in an ashtray on the shelf directly above the tub. From the length of its ash, it appeared to have been abandoned not long after it had been lit.

There were traces of water on the floor, leading to the back door. This door was open as well. In the hard-packed dirt of the yard, where flowers had been planted near the cabin, he discovered two sets of mingling prints: boots and bare feet.

Stillman's heart beat faster as he followed the prints across the yard and down the grade toward the river, pocked here and there with gopher holes. A jackrabbit bolted from a sage clump. The grass was drying out. Only the soles of Stillman's boots were damp. The killer had been chasing the woman, running full out, for the indentations his boots had left in the ground were deep and widely spaced.

Stillman imagined the woman's horror—chased through a dark pasture at night by a knife-wielding killer. She'd no doubt run this way, toward the river, hoping to find help from some camping drifter. She must have screamed, but the wind had been blowing. Chances anyone had heard were slim.

After Stillman had walked about a hundred feet, he pulled up short. Both sets of tracks disappeared in torn, matted weeds and blood. Lots of blood, crimson in the morning light. Small spatters of it were turning brown.

The killer had caught up to her here and killed her. Then he'd dragged her into the thick shrubs along the river to hide her, in case anyone had heard her scream.

Stillman's knees quaked and his heart thumped. He felt mildly sick, as though he'd chugged a glass of sour milk. It had been a long time since he'd seen that much blood.

He stood there for a long time, mulling it over, trying to envision it all, trying to distance himself from the horror and remain objective. At the same time he tried to suppress his feelings of inadequacy. Bar fights, spontaneous shootings, horse thieves, cattle rustlers, and bank robbers he could handle. That's pretty much all he'd had to confront in his twenty years as a lawman. Most of the dozen or so murders he'd encountered were bar and street shootings between drunk cowboys, with plenty of witnesses. All Stillman had had to do was walk up, remove the smoking guns from the killers' hands, and throw the culprits in the hoosegow.

Now he had two murder victims and a killer still at large.

Okay, he calmed himself. *Steady. Think.*

He steadied himself. He thought. He walked back to the cabin and looked around. Then he went back over to the barn and scrutinized the murder scene there, looking around and trying to imagine how it had looked in the darkness, a cool wind blowing, the sky full of stars.

He noticed weeds broken and matted near the barn. Walking over, he discovered a cigarette butt. He picked it up and inspected it. The tobacco and paper were not dry enough to be very old. He closed his hand over the butt and walked to the white frame house that sat about two hundred feet catty-corner from the barn, with a lean-to woodshed in which a passel of kittens played among the split stove wood and a washtub.

Stillman knocked on the door. Tollefson answered it. The smell of bacon wafted through the open doorway.

"Do you smoke, Gunther?" Stillman asked.

The farmer frowned. "Huh?"

Stillman opened his hand, revealing the quirley

stub. The paper had loosened, spilling tobacco. "You smoke these?"

Tollefson shook his head and put his hand on the pipe bowl protruding from the breast pocket of his overalls. *"Nein.* Just da pipe I smoke. Vy?"

Brow furrowed in thought, Stillman turned and headed back to the barn. He walked around the blood-splattered weeds, hands in his back pockets, lips pursed, thinking. Then he went back through the cabin again. He sat down at the small table where the woman had probably prepared her meals. He got out his makings and rolled a cigarette. Smoking, he went over it all again in his head.

The killer had chased her out of the cabin. She was naked, so she must have been bathing just before he'd started chasing her. The open doors meant the killer wasn't a customer. She wouldn't be "working" with the doors open. For the same reason, the killer hadn't been in the tub with her. He'd come in one of those doors, probably the front door, surprising her. She'd scrambled out of the tub and run. He'd caught her near the river and killed her.

Stillman walked to the door through which the killer had entered. He tossed down his cigarette, mashed it out with his boot, and walked toward town, straight across Gunther Tollefson's pasture. On First Street, near the jailhouse, he changed his mind and headed for the Drovers Saloon. As he'd figured, Doc Evans was there, sitting at a table in the shadows, drinking a beer with tomato juice. His eyes were darkly contemplative. They rose as Stillman approached.

"What are you doing here, Sheriff?" he said dryly. "Shouldn't you be out trying to find the killer?"

"I am." Stillman pulled out a chair and sat down. "Tell me what you know about Cadena Martin and the drummer."

The doctor forced a wry smile. "She had a lovely pair of breasts and was surprisingly athletic in bed. He was a quiet man and could play a mediocre game of five-card stud."

"How often did you visit her?"

Evans shrugged. "Once a week—usually on a weeknight. She was busy on weekends. Popular with the older gents who can get it up once every seven days, and those who didn't want their secrets spread around town. You could always count on Cadena not to spread secrets."

"What was she like?"

"Me."

"Pardon?"

"She was the cynical bitch to my cynical son of a bitch. We complemented each other well—for the hour or two we were together each week. Some of the girls—especially the younger ones—like to pretend they give a damn. Well, Cadena never pretended to give a damn. At least not with me. That's what she liked about me. That's what I liked about her."

Evans sipped his beer thoughtfully and continued.

"She'd been married to a hard Cajun, who'd dragged her north when she was fourteen. She ended up killing him in self-defense, changing her name, and running from the law. She tried making a 'respectable' living for a while, but gave it up after she was dragged under a railroad bridge and repeatedly raped. It soured her even more than her old man had soured her. So she took to the streets, working in brothels in several different cow towns. She was a go-getter, though, and decided she didn't like having to share her take each night with a madam.

"She saved a little money, hopped the train, thought Clantick looked as good as anywhere to drive in a stake, and moved into the old trapper's cabin. Was doing a fine business, too."

Stillman sat back in his chair, arms folded, and pondered the information.

"What about the drummer?" he asked at length.

"I hadn't seen him since his last trip to town. I didn't know he frequented Cadena. Like I said, she was tight-lipped about her customers."

Stillman sighed. "Well, I'm sorry."

The doctor looked at him emotionlessly. "Why?"

"Cadena. Obviously you cared for her."

"I cared for her body," Evans said with a dry chuckle. "Nothing more, nothing less."

Stillman stared at the man. Since meeting Evans six months ago, he'd always wondered what had made the man so cynical. He knew he'd come from a family of doctors, that he'd wanted to be an En-

glish teacher but had deferred to his father's wishes
and gone to medical school, and that he'd come west
not long after finishing his internship in Pennsylvania. He'd never married, he read the classics,
drank himself comatose every night, and made no
secret of his predilection for brothels.

Could he be the killer? Could his denial of any
feelings for Cadena Martin be an attempt to throw
Stillman off his track? He was a doctor and an undertaker, so he was certainly adept with a knife.

"Whatever you say, Doc," Stillman said, standing
and turning toward the door.

"Sheriff," Evans said.

Stillman looked at him. "You'll want to watch
yourself. If the killer's still in town, and if he thinks
you might be getting close to finding him . . ."

Stillman tried to read the man's inscrutable eyes.
Had he just been given a warning? He reflected that
he'd known the man for six months and hardly knew
him at all. He wondered if a lifetime would be long
enough.

"I'll watch my back," Stillman said finally, and
left.

5

STILLMAN LET THE batwings swing shut behind him and stopped on the boardwalk with a sigh. He glanced to his right down First Street, where Jeff Carney was approaching in his wheelchair, Sweets in tow. The horse's reins were tied to the chair. The muscles in Carney's yoke-sized shoulders bulged every time he planted his big hands on the wheels of the chair and gave them a spin.

"Hey there, Jeff," Stillman said, stepping off the boardwalk. "I could've walked over and picked him up."

"Mr. Hall down the street said he saw you walk in here," Carney said. "It's no problem. It's time for my beer break, anyway."

"Well, I thank you mighty kindly. What do I owe you?"

"One dollar." The crippled man produced a small piece of paper from his pocket. "Here's the note for the town council."

Stillman stuffed a hand in his pants pocket and produced a silver dollar. "Here's your dollar," he said, tossing it to the blacksmith. Carney caught the coin in one hand and offered the horse's reins with the other. "If we wait for the politicians, you won't get paid till spring."

"Much obliged," he said. "Say, I been wondering . . . who got killed?"

"The mulatto," Stillman said. "Cadena Martin. And a drummer from out of town."

"*Two* people?"

"That's right," Stillman said darkly.

"Any idea who killed them?"

"None at the moment, Jeff. I'm workin' on it."

Carney thought for a moment, then tipped back his head to look up at Stillman, scrunching one eye closed. His thin, pewter hair curled back from a pronounced widow's peak, and he was black with soot. "Sounds like a crime of passion, you ask me."

"It does at that, doesn't it?"

Carney swung his chair around with a flick of his arms, and Stillman helped him onto the boardwalk. "Obliged," the blacksmith said, wheeling through the batwings. "And good luck."

"Thanks, Jeff. I reckon I'm gonna need it."

Stillman stepped off the boardwalk and headed across the street to the Windsor Hotel. He tied Sweets to the hitchrack outside and stepped through the glass doors, which a girl was cleaning, and asked the manager, Mr. Lang, if a drummer by the name of Reginald Dawson had bought a room last night. Lang ran his ringed pinky finger down his register book and shook his head. "Nope, but I recognize the name. He's been here before. I think he switches off between us and Mrs. Adams's place up the street. You might check there, Sheriff."

"Thanks," Stillman said, turning for the door.

"What's he done, anyway?" Lang called after him.

"Got himself killed," Stillman said without turning. The girl cleaning the doors turned to him sharply, and Stillman tipped his hat to her.

Five minutes later, Stillman mounted the steps of the Boston Hotel. With three stories, a balcony on each floor, and a big, airy lobby with a stone fireplace and Oriental rugs, the Boston was the best hotel in town. Pricey, too, with rooms going for three-fifty a night. The drummer must have had a hell of an expense account.

Stillman learned from Thomas Adams, the proprietor, that Dawson had indeed bought a room, just after the last train of the day pulled into town.

"Was he alone?" Stillman asked.

Adams nodded. "He wasn't up there more than two minutes, though, before he left. I figured he must've had an appointment with a drink somewhere . . . though I serve the best booze in town," Adams said with a thick-fingered twist of his waxed mustache.

"What time did he leave?" Stillman asked.

"Oh, I'd say it was around ten-thirty, eleven. The train was due in at ten, so yeah, I'd say around ten-thirty. Never showed up again. You know what happened to him, Ben?"

"He's dead," Stillman said with an air of distraction. "Can I have his room key?"

"Who killed him?" Adams said, turning and reaching for a key on one of the many gold hooks behind him.

"Don't know yet," Stillman said. He grabbed the key out of the hotel owner's fat hand, turned, and headed for the stairs across the lobby.

"Well, you have any ideas?"

"None," Stillman lied. He wasn't about to tell the man he suspected the doctor. He hadn't really even admitted that to himself yet.

Stillman climbed the stairs, walked down the hall lit only by the single window at the far end, and turned the key in the lock of Room 17, twisting the knob and pushing open the door. The room was standard Boston fare, nearly twice as large as any other room in town, and boasting heavy drapes over the windows and a big soft bed with a high oak headboard. The drummer had been in a hurry to drop off his bags, it appeared, for a suitcase and carpetbag sat on the bed, propped against each other, unopened. An expensive-looking umbrella lay over the suitcase.

The mulatto must have met the man's train. Stillman had often seen her at the station house, sitting on one of the stiff-backed benches, reading the paper and waiting for the next locomotive to chug into town. She knew when her regulars arrived and was always there to meet them—mostly drummers and other traveling businessmen, taking advantage of their time away from home for a little illicit sex with a discreet professional.

The mulatto's meeting with Dawson had probably been prearranged, and she no doubt had waited outside the Boston for him while he checked into his room, then drove him over to the old trapper's cabin, where she plied her trade. Apparently Dawson hadn't wanted to be seen with her or wanted anyone to see her visit his room. Probably a "good" Christian, happily married man with a liberal dose of Calvinistic modesty, at least enough to compel him to keep his prurient behavior discreet.

Stillman looked around the room. Finding nothing unusual, he grabbed the drummer's bags and umbrella off the bed and headed downstairs. In the lobby he informed Adams he'd taken possession of the dummer's luggage and headed over to the jailhouse, where he set it on his desk. He stood back and stared at it, giving a sigh. Having a dead man's personal effects in his possession made him feel haunted, but he knew he had to go through them on the off chance they might contain a clue as to who might have killed the man, or why.

He removed his corduroy jacket, draped it over his chair back, rolled up his shirtsleeves, and opened the carpetbag, dipping his hand inside and pulling out one article at a time. When he had both bags emptied, and everything lay in stacks on his desk—carefully folded trousers, perfumed dress shirt, silk pajamas, fine cotton underwear, and a handful of toiletries including a mustache comb and ivory toothbrush—he sat back in his chair with a tired groan.

The door opened and Leon McMannigle walked in. The deputy closed the door on the din of passing drays and ranch wagons. "Startin' to get busy out there," he said conversationally, hanging his hat on a wall peg by the door. He turned to Stillman, who was deep in thought and staring at the articles on his desk.

"What you got there?" Leon asked.

Stillman told him.

"Find anything worthwhile?"

"Not a thing."

"Well, you didn't really expect to, did you?"

"I was hoping I'd turn up something, but it looks like the poor man was in the wrong place at the wrong time." Stillman sighed raggedly. "And now I'm going to have to cable his family and tell them he's dead."

"What are you gonna tell 'em?" Leon asked, gathering kindling from the wood box near the stove.

Stillman thought for a moment. "That he was out having a smoke in the back alley when someone stabbed him. How does that sound?"

"Sounds good to me," Leon said, snapping a piece of kindling over his knee. "No use hurting them with the truth when you don't have to."

Stillman got up and started packing the drummer's possessions back in the bags. "You come up with anything?" he asked his deputy, knowing that Leon had done some investigating of his own.

McMannigle was not a trained lawman, but as a soldier in the black Tenth Cavalry, he'd tracked and fought Apaches in Arizona and had developed a talent for investigation. Stillman had personally offered him the deputy's job when the Clantick city council had asked Stillman to be sheriff. Stillman had first met the black man when Stillman was on the Hi-Line hunting rustlers and the killer of his old hide-hunting partner, Bill Harmon.

Leon started a fire in the stove, set the percolator to boil, and sat in the chair on the other side of Stillman's desk. He hiked a spurred boot on his knee, shaking his head. "I visited all three flop-houses in town and talked to most of the girls. None had heard of any dude who'd gotten all starry-eyed over Cadena and wanted her all for himself. They also didn't know of anyone who had it in for her. Last but not least, none knew of the drummer." He nodded at the luggage Stillman was setting on the floor beside his desk.

Stillman sat back in his chair, making it squeak. "Yeah, I have a feeling our traveling salesman was a regular with the mulatto and only the mulatto."

"Her customers were loyal—I'll say that for her."

Stillman racked his brain, thinking. "Any trouble-makers in town? No accounts who like to slap women around?"

Leon sighed and scratched his head. "I think we done spooked all the troublemakers out of town, Ben."

"Not all of them," Stillman said.

"No, I guess not."

Stillman thought for a long time. The coffee gurgled on the stove. The fire snapped. Out on the street, someone yelled for Danny to get his ass down to the blacksmith shop pronto. For Stillman, the sounds came from a long way away.

"Well, she had to be the target," he said, entwining his hands on his chest and steepling his index fingers against his chin. "If the drummer had been the target, the killer would have killed only him and left Cadena alone. But he didn't. First he killed the drummer, and then he went looking for Cadena. We know he wasn't after money, because the drummer had a wallet full of cash. And the mulatto's cabin hasn't been ransacked. I'm guessing the killer just happened into the drummer along the trail and killed him so he couldn't identify him."

"That sounds right."

"Where does it leave us?"

"I reckon it leaves us lookin' for a motive," Leon said.

"And that isn't gonna be easy, since Miss Martin

kept to herself." Stillman sighed and stood. Thoughtfully, he rolled down his shirtsleeves and buttoned them, then donned his hat and headed for the door.

"Well, I think I'll check all the stables and livery barns," he said halfheartedly. "See if any strangers have stabled their horses here lately. Then I'll telegraph the man's family, offer to ship his body on the train. Why don't you check the train and the rest of the hotels?"

"Ben?" Leon said as Stillman opened the door to the midday clatter of horses and wagons and laughing cowpokes.

Stillman turned back to his deputy, whose eyes were troubled. "This son of a bitch could be long gone by now, couldn't he?"

"He could."

"I sure hope he ain't. Cadena was a fine woman who didn't deserve half o' what she got. Seems like the least we should do is find her killer."

"We will," Stillman said, resolutely. "We will."

Two nights later, Hansel Hagen retired to a chair near the woodstove in the cabin he'd built along Box Elder Creek, four miles south of Clantick. While his wife and two young daughters cleared the table and washed the dishes, and while the baby slept in its cradle, Hansel picked his teeth and tried to figure out how he was going to feed and clothe the third child his wife Kirsti had recently informed him she was carrying in her womb.

He sat in his chair and thought about it for a long time, hearing the wind howl around the cabin—the cabin he'd have to add another room to next spring. He stuffed his pipe and smoked it.

Hansel was twenty-five years old. He and Kirsti had married five years ago and homesteaded these acres after arriving on the Hi-Line from Minot, in western Dakota. First, they'd built a sod shanty. Then, when their second daughter was born, Hansel and two neighbors built the cabin. He'd thought the two-story log dwelling would last him a good ten or fifteen years. But now, in light of another bun in Kirsti's oven, it just wouldn't do.

As young as Hansel was, he was tired. His back, neck, and legs ached constantly from trying to tear a living out of this stubborn sod. He just didn't have the energy to add another room to the cabin. He wished Kirsti would never have let him crawl between her legs after the dance over at Johs's barn, when Hansel had drunk too much chokecherry wine—nothing made him randier! He hoped she'd have enough good sense in the future to keep her legs together when he was drunk.

Hadn't she learned her lesson? He'd learned his, by God! Enough was enough! He couldn't go adding another room to the cabin every year!

Hansel shook his head and pushed himself to his feet, feeling owly and embittered. He'd spent his whole life working to get ahead but seemed to only fall farther and farther behind.

Finally, when Kirsti and the girls had finished cleaning the kitchen, Hansel knocked the dottle from his pipe, pushed his young, tired body out of the creaky rocker, and stretched.

"I'm going to check on the stock," he muttered, taking his tattered wool coat off its peg by the door, then pulling it on.

Kirsti was busy gathering her darning, which would keep her occupied for the next hour or so, and didn't bother answering him. She knew as well as Hansel did that "going out to check the stock" meant going out to drink the homemade busthead their neighbor, Baldric Ingelmann, distilled behind his well house.

Pulling the cabin door shut behind him, Hansel lifted his collar up. The wind was chilly, not as unseasonably balmy as it had been, and the sky was full of stars. It would probably freeze tonight, and Hansel would have to break the ice in the water troughs.

Heading for the barn, he cursed and spat at the thought of another winter laying in—another five months of slogging through knee-deep snow to feed his stock, another five months of constant woodsplitting to feed the stoves. Five months of being imprisoned right here on the farm, listening to his wife grouch, his kids scream, and the brittle wind moan in the chimney. He felt a glimmer of hope, thinking of the occasional dances at Johs's barn, where he'd visit with his neighbors, eye the older girls, swill chokecherry wine, and forget about all the ways his life hadn't turned out the way he'd expected it to when he was a kid.

Hansel heaved the barn door open and stepped inside, fishing for the box of quirleys in his pocket. He felt around for the lantern on the joist. Finding it, he lifted the chimney, trimmed and lit the wick, and held the lamp high as he made his way down the alley. The buttery light tilted shadows across the hay and mangers, revealing the singletrees, collars, halters, and wood-handled tools hanging from beams. The milch cow mooed a greeting. The air was heavy with the smell of dung and ammonia. Mice scuttled.

Hansel hung the lamp on a joist, opened the oat bin, and fished around for his bottle. He gave a satisfied grunt when his hand felt its cool smoothness. Bringing it out of the oats, he shut the lid and sat on it. Hiking a wood-soled boot on his knee, he uncorked the bottle and grinned, staring at the lip, smelling the sharp, honeylike aroma of the raw alcohol.

Something moved in the hay of one of the stalls. Something big.

Hansel raised his eyes and saw a large shadow slide across the floor. The shadow jerked against the wall to Hansel's right, and a man came into the lantern light.

Hansel was too startled to move.

"Hello, Hansel," a deep voice said. It was a cold voice, more chill than the wind outside. "Share a drink with an old friend?"

6

THE NEXT MORNING at eight A.M., Fay Stillman arranged her papers on her desk in the one-room schoolhouse in Clantick, then walked out to the front porch and rang the bell. Instantly, the children on the playground—nine boys and twelve girls—stopped their games to regard Fay miserably.

"Ah, teacher, cain't we have just one more minute?" Johnny Larson begged, scrunching up his eyes.

"Not even one," Fay said, throwing her head back with a laugh.

Every morning her eight o'clock bell got the same response. She might have taken it personally had she not remembered having the same reaction when she was a little girl, attending a small school five miles south of her father's ranch near the Yellowstone River. Fay had only attended school for the first four years, however, as the area ranchers hadn't been able to keep a teacher in so remote a place. After that, Fay's education had been up to her classically educated French parents, and then to herself.

"Ah, Teacher," Johnny complained, ending his game of marbles and moving with the other students to the school's front door, where Fay waited with her bell, complimenting the girls on their dresses and the boys on their shoe shines.

"Don't worry, Johnny, you're going to have fun today," Fay teased as the boy passed. "We're going to start the morning with your favorite subject—English!"

"Ah, *Teacher*!" the boy cried.

Fay laughed and tousled the boy's blond hair. She was about to pull the door closed when something caught her eye, and she gave her gaze to the street. A small, green box wagon rattled up to the hitching post. The wagon was driven by a small, pale woman in a red scarf. Beside her sat a young girl who Fay recognized as Candace Hawley.

Fay stepped off the porch as Candace and her mother approached Fay on the path.

"Candace, Mrs. Hawley—you don't know how happy I am to see you!" Fay said, taking the timid girl's hands in hers and regarding her mother with a heartfelt smile.

"She wanted to come so bad . . . and she seems to like you so much, Mrs. Stillman, that . . . well, I finally got Earl to let her come."

"I'm so pleased you did, Mrs. Hawley. Candace, welcome back!"

The brown-eyed ten-year-old made a feeble attempt at a smile, then bolted past Fay and into the school.

Fay turned to the woman, who wrung her small, work-roughened hands together before her modest bosom. Fay was about to thank the woman again for bringing Candace to school, when she saw Mrs. Hawley's bruised right eye.

"Oh!" Fay said, startled. "Mrs. Hawley . . . your eye—does it hurt?"

Suddenly nervous, the woman shook her head and smiled, backing away. "Oh . . . it's . . . it's not nothin'," she said. "Just fell down the stairs the other night, when I got up to use the privy. It'll heal." She stopped and regarded Fay directly. "I do want to thank you for comin' over to the house the other night and askin' Earl to let Candace come to school regular. I know he wouldn't have even considered it if only me and Candace asked him. He just feels funny about his daughter gettin' educated, you know . . . since he never learned to write and cipher his ownself"—The woman turned away shyly— "and . . . and I didn't neither."

"Well, it was Candace who asked me to step in," Fay said. "That's how much she really wants to learn. And she has a brain for it, too. Your daughter is a very lovely and intelligent young woman, and while I know she has chores to do at home, I really believe it would be a shame if she didn't receive a formal education. It would be a great loss to Candace as well as to you and your husband, Mrs. Hawley."

"Well, there she is. She's all yours. For today, anyway. I think we just have to take it one day at a time, Mrs. Stillman." The woman turned and headed back toward the wagon.

"You and your husband won't regret it, I assure you, Mrs. Hawley," Fay called to her.

She stood on the footpath and watched Mrs. Hawley climb into the wagon, flap the reins against the horse's back, and rattle away—probably back to her farm and a boiler full of clothes to wash or floors to sweep. Or lunch to prepare for her silent, arbitrary husband who treated his family little better than his livestock, as was evidenced by Mrs. Hawley's blackened eye.

As Fay walked toward the school, she hoped her visit to the Hawley farm the other night hadn't instigated the violence Earl Hawley had dealt his poor, long-suffering wife. But Fay had had no alternative. When Candace had visited her in tears the other day, saying her father refused to let her return to school, Fay felt a visit with Mr. and Mrs. Hawley was imperative.

Earl Hawley had mostly just grunted and fidgeted in his chair, not speaking more than two complete sentences, so Fay had had no idea what the outcome of her visit might be. Until now. He might have taken out a little frustration on his wife, but at least his lovely, gifted, albeit timid, daughter was back in school where she belonged.

Feeling grateful for that, Fay returned to the classroom, where Candace Hawley had taken her usual seat, looking suddenly very proud and happy, small hands entwined on her desk, ready to learn. The room was buzzing, alive with energy, and it took Fay several minutes to get the children settled down and to channel their energy into the morning's English assignment.

When she'd given the class a topic and had allowed the children a half hour to write, she called on volunteers to read what they had written. Fay was thrilled to see Candace Hawley's hand dart up first, shaking with eager excitement.

"Can I read mine, Mrs. Stillman? Can I, can I?"

Fay smiled and nodded, trying to maintain her professional reserve. "Go ahead, Candace."

Fay was so pleased by the girl's presence in the class that she had trouble concentrating on the math lesson which followed English. During recess, she brewed a pot of coffee on the stove and sipped it sitting on the outside steps, where she watched the children play. Candace and two other girls were skipping rope and so deeply involved in boisterous, selfless conversation that Fay was doubly pleased with herself for getting Candace back in school. Only in school, around other children, and challenged and stimulated by books and learning, did Candace seem to lose her timidity and fear, which had no doubt been the result of living with a hard, unloving father.

It was almost as though Fay's thinking of the man had produced him, for there he was, driving the green buckboard wagon toward the school. His dark, unshaven face was hidden by the floppy brim of his tattered felt hat. He was a tall, lean man, all knees and elbows and oversized feet in lace-up farm boots. His pinstriped overalls were yellow with old grease and dirt stains.

He pulled up at the hitchrack before the playground, and Fay's ears hummed with apprehension. Her heart throbbed. She glanced at Candace, who had frozen in play to stare at the man, who set the buckboard's brake and climbed clumsily off the wagon, staggering a little.

Fay set down her coffee cup and hurried out to meet the man at the start of the footpath. Feeling apprehensive but trying to remain calm, she said, "Good morning, Mr. Hawley."

He stopped in front of the hitchrack and aimed his pale gray eyes at her like gun barrels. "Mornin', nothin'. I come fer my daughter."

He moved to step around Fay, and she quickly stepped in his path. "Why—is something wrong?"

"Yeah, I'll say somethin's wrong," Hawley groused, exhaling the sweet smell of beer and rye whiskey. "My daughter's playin' out here like some moron when she should be home muckin' out the barn stalls."

With a gruff hand, he pushed Fay aside and made a beeline for his daughter, who stood staring at him with speechless, tight-lipped horror, tears filling her eyes. The other students had stopped their play, as well, and watched the man curiously.

"Come on—let's go," he ordered Candace, taking her by the arm and jerking her toward the wagon.

"But, Pa, you said—"

"I don't care what I said; I changed my mind. You got work at home. Sk'daddle!"

Casting a helpless gaze at Fay, the girl slumped toward the wagon. Halfway there she lowered her chin, and her face crumpled as she cried.

Fay hurried over to the man, positioning herself between the farmer and the wagon, resting her hands on Candace's quivering shoulders. "Mr. Hawley, please, you can't do this. Your wife just brought Candace here a few hours ago, and—"

"I don't care what my wife said. My daughter ain't got time to play dress-up. She's got chores to do at home."

Fay was flabbergasted. "That's what you think school is, Mr. Hawley? Dress up?"

"That's exac'ly what I think it is. Now kindly get out of my way."

"I can't let you do this to your daughter, Mr. Hawley. School means too much to her, and your wife said you agreed to let her attend."

"Get your hands off my daughter and step aside, woman," Hawley said menacingly.

Fay looked at Candace, who'd covered her face with her hands and was bawling uncontrollably. "Candace, why don't you go into the school so your father and I can talk?"

"I said get out of my way, woman!" Hawley yelled, reaching out and shoving Fay so abruptly aside that Fay tripped on the hem of her dress and fell, scraping her hands on the rocky, hard-packed ground.

"Teacher!" yelled Johnny Larson, who came running to Fay's side. "Are you okay, Teacher?" All the other students came running as well.

"I'm okay, Johnny," Fay said, turning onto her butt and regarding the scraped palms of her hands.

"Mrs. Stillman, you're bleeding," one of the older girls said.

"It's all right, Laura. Everyone, into the school. Please, go inside."

As the children turned to obey—all but Johnny Larson, that is, who had a crush on his pretty teacher—Fay climbed to her feet in time to see Earl Hawley slap the reins against his horse's back and canter off down the street, his jaw set in a rigid line, eyes straight ahead, Candace crying beside him on the wagon seat.

Johnny stooped to pick up a rock and ran into the street behind the wagon. "You rotten old fart!" the boy screamed, slinging the stone, which thudded off the wagon box. "How dare you hit my teacher!"

"Johnny!" Fay called. "Come back here this *second!*"

The wagon stopped and Earl Hawley twisted around to look behind him. "Come here, kid," he called dangerously.

"You hit my teacher, you rotten old dog!" Johnny screamed from the middle of the street.

"Johnny!" Fay yelled, running toward the boy.

"Come here, kid," Hawley said. He held up his right fist, clenched so tightly it was red. "I wanna tell ya a little secret."

Fay grabbed Johnny by the shoulders and pushed him toward the school. "Johnny Larson, you listen to me," she yelled, her voice quaking with emotion. "Get inside!"

Finally, Johnny obeyed, running toward the schoolhouse. Fay turned to the wagon. Candace was bent over her knees with her head in her hands. Hawley was still twisted around in his seat, looking behind him at Fay. It was a dark, menacing look that turned even more eerie when a light entered the man's eyes. He was *leering* at her.

And just then Fay realized the kind of man she was dealing with.

When Hawley turned back around and drove away, Fay slouched over to the hitchrack and placed both hands and most of her weight on it, and tried to calm her nerves. It didn't work. Her teeth ground angrily together as she imagined the violence she wanted to inflict on Earl Hawley.

She'd known some stupid, cruel men in her day, but none as stupid and cruel as Earl Hawley.

When she'd gotten herself together, she walked into the school and canceled class for the rest of the day. She had too much on her mind. She had to do something about Earl Hawley.

7

WHEN THE DAY had first begun, Ben Stillman and Leon McMannigle were having breakfast in Sam Wa's Café. They were giving a playful hard time to Evelyn Vincent, the former pleasure girl from Helena whom Stillman had helped land the job as Sam Wa's only waitress. Evelyn had told them they were both impossible and had headed back to the kitchen, when hooves thundered past the big, plate-glass window.

Turning toward the street, Stillman saw Ferd Borrow, a farmer from south of town, rein his strawberry roan to a halt before the jailhouse and dismount in a hurry.

"Well, what do you s'pose that's all about?" Stillman asked McMannigle.

"I don't know, but it sure looks urgent. Want me to go see, Ben?"

"No, I finished my eggs. You're still working on yours." Stillman wiped his mouth with his napkin, donned his hat, scraped his chair back, and headed for the door.

When he'd stepped out on the boardwalk and looked toward the jailhouse, Borrow was pounding on the jailhouse's locked door. "We're over here, Ferd," Stillman called to the man.

When the farmer turned, Stillman waved. Borrow grabbed his horse's reins and jogged across the street. He was out of breath when he approached Stillman, and his eyes were distressed.

"What's the matter, Ferd? What's happened?"

"It's Hansel Hagen," the tall, heavy-shouldered man said. He wore a visored, deerskin watch cap and a blue, mice-chewed mackinaw. His bushy auburn mustache drew down around his mouth, moist with sweat though it was only in the high forties. It was apparent the man had galloped all six miles from his farm. The strawberry roan was lathered like it was June.

Borrow swallowed with effort, bobbing his head. "Hansel . . . he's . . . he's dead."

"How?"

"I dunno. His wife rode over to my place this morning with her kids, screaming and shrieking like she was in labor or something. When Lisa got her calmed down, she said she found Hansel in the barn, dead. Kilt . . . murdered."

"Murdered?" Stillman grunted, feeling his scalp tighten ominously.

"I didn't go over . . . I didn't look. I just saddled up and came to town to get you."

Leon had stepped onto the boardwalk and come up behind Stillman, who turned to him now. "I guess we'd better ride out there," Stillman said.

"I'll get the horses," Leon said, heading across the street to the jail, in the back of which was a lean-to shed and small corral where they kept their mounts.

"Meet us at Auld's," Stillman told him. "We have to get Ferd here another horse. He rides that roan anymore this morning, he'll kill it."

Fifteen minutes later they were on the wagon road angling south of Clantick, along the twisting, tree- and brush-lined Box Elder Creek. It was a breezy, sunny autumn day, but the chill threatened winter. Leaves blew across the trail and hawks quarreled in the occasional box elders. The three men rode hard but not as hard as Borrow had ridden on his way into town. Stillman and McMannigle needed to save their mounts for the return journey.

On the way, Stillman tried to get more information from the stunned farmer, but all Borrow seemed to know was what he'd reported in town: Hansel Hagen's wife had found him dead in his barn. Murdered. That was it.

Nearly an hour after they'd left Clantick, Still- man, McMannigle, and Ferd Borrow rounded a bend in the road, bringing up several gray, weather- beaten buildings and a corral. Chickens pecked in the yard and several hogs snorted in a pen behind the corral. The air was rife with their fetid odor. Stillman led the group to the barn, where all three men dismounted and tied their mounts to the corral.

"Here we go," Stillman said with a sigh and opened one of the two big doors. He took an involuntary step back. "Holy Christ!"

The other two men followed his startled gaze to the inside of the door, to which Hansel Hagen had been pinned with a pitchfork.

"Lordy God almighty!" Leon cooed, black eyes wide as silver dollars. "You didn't tell us they forked him to the galldang *door!*"

Borrow was too busy retching to reply.

Stillman approached the body, scrutinizing it. Hansel's eyes were lightly closed and his head was tipped to a shoulder. There was a deep, wide gash across his throat, stretching from one earlobe to the other.

"Just like the other one," Leon said, reading his mind. "Just like the mulatto."

"The mulatto wasn't pitchforked afterward," Stillman said.

"Yeah, but the knife gash is the same."

Stillman nodded his head reluctantly. It would be too much of a coincidence for two killers to kill the same way, within two days of each other. It did indeed look as though young Hansel had been murdered by the same person who'd murdered Cadena Martin.

But why?

Stillman turned to Ferd Borrow, sitting on a hay bale outside the corral, elbows on his knees, head bent over his hands. Stillman walked over to him and sat down beside him. "Hansel have any enemies, Ferd?"

Borrow shook his head. "None that I knew about."

"He get into any arguments lately?" Stillman continued desperately. "Maybe seen his wife with some other man? Maybe just saw another man making eyes at her? She's not a bad looking woman, if I remember correctly."

"If he did, I didn't know about it, and I seen him just yesterday. He wasn't worked up about nothin' except winter comin' on and his wife carryin' another kid. But he wasn't worked up really. Just"— Borrow shrugged—"you know, concerned."

Stillman shook his head, knowing the questions were useless but continuing just the same, hoping against hope that the same person had not committed both murders. If the same person had indeed, then Stillman had a serial killer on his hands: a crafty, elusive madman who enjoyed what he did and would no doubt do it again.

"He sell any cows to anyone lately, Ferd? Or any hay?"

"Didn't tell me if he did," Borrow said.

"You see anyone ride this way last night? Maybe

a neighbor coming over with a bottle? Something like that?"

"Nope."

"Well, goddamn it, Ferd, what in the hell *can* you tell me?"

Borrow rolled his head to one side, giving Stillman his sad, stricken eyes. "Just what I told you in town, Sheriff. That's all I can tell you."

Leon stepped out of the barn and jerked his head, beckoning Stillman. Then he went back inside the barn.

Stillman found him at the other end of the alley, before the oat bin. It was semidark back here, the light from the two open doors barely penetrating. Flies buzzed around broken glass on the floor. "What's that?" Stillman said.

"Whiskey bottle. Looks to me, from the prints in the hay and dirt, that Hansel was in here drinkin', and the killer surprised him. Might've been waitin' for him. Maybe they scuffled around a little. By the looks of some of those tracks, I'd say the killer backed him all the way to the other end of the barn, cut his throat, and while he was still standin' there, dyin', pinned him to the door with the pitchfork. Must be a strong bastard."

He and Stillman strolled back along the alley, eyes on the scuffed hay on the barn floor. When they came to the body still suspended on the door, which creaked back and forth with the breeze, sliding Hansel's sandy, cropped hair across his pale blue forehead, Stillman lifted his eyes to his deputy, pursing his lips.

"Good detective work," he said wryly.

"Who you s'pose this son of a bitch is, Ben? Why did he kill these two people? What's the connection?"

"I haven't the foggiest idea," Stillman said. "There has to be one, though. They have to be related. If it was just some madman killing willy-nilly, it doesn't figure he'd go to all the trouble of coming out here, to this isolated farm. He'd stay in town, where the pickin's aren't so thin and there are more places to hide."

He scratched his chin and leaned against a joist. "I'm at my wits' end, Leon. I really am."

"We'll get him, Ben. You said so yourself."

"But how many people is he going to kill before we do?"

Both men were silent and fidgety. Both were highly competitive, and neither liked to get beat. But they were both getting beat bad and, even more frustrating, they were getting beat by an unseen enemy. Someone had killed two people and then disappeared, slinked off in the shadows to laugh at the two men whose jobs it was to find him.

The only way they'd find him was to find out why he was killing. But so far, they didn't have a clue. They'd had only one possibility, and that was that the man had been in love with Cadena Martin and had killed her because she'd refused him. He'd killed the drummer simply because he'd gotten in the way. At first, Stillman had considered the doctor. In spite of his hard, cynical facade, the man had obviously felt something for the whore.

But now, with the death of Hansel Hagen, who lived four miles from town and could have little or no personal connection with Cadena Martin, there was no reason to believe the murders were crimes of passion or that the doctor was involved. There had to be someone, some*thing* else—but what? Who?

"It's got to be someone from around here," Stillman said.

"How's that?"

"Drifters come and go. They don't linger. If they do, we notice them and inquire about their business. But I haven't seen any drifters around here lately. At least none that have stayed but a night or two. No, this guy's *from* here. I have a feeling we see him every day. That's why he's invisible."

Leon nodded. He'd rolled a quirley and was smoking it thoughtfully. "Makes sense."

"Why don't you head on back to town, and watch things there, in case he decides to strike again. He could very well do that, if he knows where we are, and I have a feeling he does. I'm going to help Ferd get Hansel's body ready for burial, and dig a grave. But first I'm going to ride around the farm and see if I can pick up any tracks. Maybe I'll get lucky and be able to track the bastard down. If not, I'll ride over to Borrow's place and talk to Hagen's widow, see if she can offer any helpful information."

"All right," Leon said, heading for his horse. "But you watch yourself, Ben. We got a killer on the loose, and I wouldn't doubt it a bit if he's not above shootin' a lawman, if he thinks his trail's been cut."

"You, too. A wolf in the fold is what he is. You're no safer in town."

McMannigle tipped his hat and trotted his horse out of the yard, the breeze whipping his dust. Stillman turned to Ferd Borrow, still sitting on the hay bale, his breakfast on the hay-flecked ground between his boots.

Stillman sighed. "Well, Ferd . . . what do you say we get ol' Hansel down?"

8

WHEN ALL THE children had left the school, celebrating as though Christmas had come in October, Fay did not linger as she normally did, tidying up the room and correcting papers. She closed the vent on the big Monarch stove, grabbed her coat and hat, locked the door behind her, and headed uptown for Ben's office.

She desperately needed her husband's advice about what to do about Earl Hawley and Candace. She knew there was probably little Ben could do legally, but Fay was certain he could offer some personal guidance. What's more, he would listen while she fumed about the morning's events, and at the moment, that's what she needed most. Ben had the most sympathetic ear of any man Fay had ever known.

That's why finding his office door locked and a note reading, Out of Town on Business—Be Back in a Few Hours, nearly buckled Fay's knees. Her heart fell with discouragement and frustration.

"Oh!" she groaned, turning from the door and clenching her fists at her sides. "Where could he have *gone?*"

"Out to the Hagen farm, Mrs. Stillman."

Fay turned to see Evelyn Vincent, the waitress from Sam Wa's, standing behind her, looking flushed and shy in her apron.

"Oh . . . hi, Evelyn," Fay said weakly.

"I saw you standing over here and thought I'd better let you know where Ben went."

"The Hagen farm, you say?" Fay inquired, puzzled.

Evelyn nodded darkly. "Ferd Borrow rode into town earlier, when Ben and Leon were having breakfast in the restaurant. I overheard Ferd tell them there'd been a murder. Hansel Hagen." The blond girl's eyes widened, drilling into Fay's, wisps of hair straying from the bun at her neck and bobbing around her face.

"Oh, my God," Fay said, for the moment forgetting about her own troubles. "That's awful."

"Isn't it, ma'am?"

"Did Ferd say who killed poor Hansel?"

"I didn't hear, ma'am. There sure has been a lot of killin' around here lately, though. I haven't see this many in this short o' time since before your husband and Leon came to town."

Fay sighed and looked away. "Yes, well . . . I hope three so close together is just a coincidence."

"Well, I just thought I'd tell you, Mrs. Stillman," Evelyn said, about to turn away.

Fay grabbed her hand in both of hers. "Thank you, Evelyn. How is everything, anyway? I've been so busy I haven't had time to stop by Sam's and see how you're doing."

Evelyn fairly beamed, her blue eyes flashing. "Just fine. I love working for Mr. Wa. He's a real gentleman, and . . . and, well, I guess you know I haven't been around too many gentlemen."

Fay knew Evelyn was referring to the gang of crooks in which Evelyn had gotten enmeshed before Ben had come to town. Two of the thieves had tried to kill Ben in his office, and they might have accomplished their task had Evelyn not gone to Ben with the information. She, Ben, and Leon had then set a trap for the would-be assassins, who were now serving lengthy sentences in the territorial pen at Deer Lodge.

Fay squeezed Evelyn's hand and gazed sincerely into her eyes. "Evelyn, my father always told me never to dwell on the mistakes of yesterday. Each day is a fresh start, a clean slate."

"Your father must be a very wise man, Mrs. Stillman."

"He was," Fay said, then added after a thought, "for the most part, that is." One of the few mistakes Alexander Beaumont had ever made was not allowing Fay to marry Ben when she'd first known the handsome deputy marshal back in Milestown. The flub had been a doozy, but Fay had forgiven her father for it, and not a day went by when she did not think of him fondly.

"Well, I best get back to work before Sam fires me," Evelyn said with a smile.

"Thanks for your help, Evelyn. And Evelyn?"

"Yes, ma'am?"

"Please call me Fay?"

Evelyn's smile grew once again. "All right . . . Fay," she said, then turned and, lifting her skirts, headed back across the street to Sam Wa's Café.

Fay watched the girl go, then turned back to the note on the door and felt her frustration return, coupled with sadness and concern over Hansel Hagen's murder. As she moved off down the boardwalk, toward her house, she wondered vaguely if there could be any connection between Hagen's murder and the murder of the mulatto woman. Fay didn't see how there could be, but three murders in three days was a lot for Clantick. Could there be a madman on the loose?

Fay shuddered to think of it as she stepped through the gate in her picket fence. Mounting the porch, she unlocked the front door of the house. Hearing the door click shut behind her, she stood in the small foyer and listened to the ensuing silence of the empty dwelling.

The harsh noon light slanting through the windows gave Fay a restless, anxious feeling, and her thoughts returned to Earl Hawley. In her mind she saw poor Candace slumped on the wagon seat, her innocent child's face buried in her hands.

Ben could be away for hours. She couldn't just sit here in this silent house, grinding her teeth over Earl Hawley. Candace had come to her with a problem, and Fay had failed the child. She had to do something. She had to do something now.

Getting an idea, she tossed her satchel on a chair, ripped her bonnet off her head, and walked resolutely into the bedroom, where she quickly changed into her riding clothes. Finding her .32 caliber Colt and cartridge belt in her dresser, she wrapped the belt around her waist, cinched it, and adjusted the oiled holster on her hip. She unsheathed the revolver, loaded it, donned her green felt riding hat and tan riding gloves, and headed out the back door for the stable and corral, where she bridled and saddled her black mare named Dorothy.

With the ease and confidence of a trained equestrian, Fay climbed into the leather and opened the corral gate with a flick of her hand. She shook her black hair out from her neck, tipped her hat brim low, and reined Dorothy around the house at a trot.

Following the streets through town, she passed log cabins, frame houses, falling-down shanties, and dead gardens. Dogs barked and leaves swirled at Dorothy's hocks. In minutes Fay shed the last privies and trash heaps of Clantick and galloped south, cross-country, down ravines and over swells, curving around sandstone crags and rocky knolls. The Two Bear Mountains loomed before her, blue green and shaggy with pines, and capped with sunlit clouds.

Fay rode with her chin up and her shoulders square, reins loose in her hands. This was where she felt her best: in the saddle, a good horse beneath her, the wind in her face, and all the wild country at her beck and call. Tempering her pleasure, however, was the evil leer of Earl Hawley and the cries of the poor, defeated Candace.

"Hold on, Candace," she said to herself. "Hold on just a little longer . . ."

Crystal Harmon slopped grease from the wooden bucket at her feet into the axle of the two-seater wagon. She scrubbed it around, applied another coat, dropped the grease stick in the bucket, wrinkling a lip at the lubricant's fetid odor, and then walked around behind the wagon and started lowering the jack.

"Crystal Harmon, just what in the hell are you doin'?"

Startled, Crystal jerked a look behind her so quickly her flat-brimmed hat fell off and her long blond hair danced around her head. Approaching her from around the barn was her husband, Jody, a slender, broad-shouldered young man with distinctly Indian features.

"By Jehovah, Jody, you startled me!"

"Answer my question," Jody demanded, moving toward her with his heavy brow furrowed in anger. He wore a black plainsman hat, canvas coat, worn blue denims, and undershot boots. From the tender way he was walking, Crystal could tell he'd come quite a ways.

"I'm greasing this here axle. What the hell does it look I'm doin'?" Crystal shot back. "Where's your horse?"

Jody stopped a few feet away from her, flushed, sweating, and breathing hard. "He spooked at a sidewinder and threw me, and then the son of a bitch run off and wouldn't come back!"

"You didn't get bit, did you?" Crystal asked, concern in her voice.

"No, I didn't get bit." Jody shoved her gently aside and finished lowering the wagon jack, until both wagon wheels were sitting firmly on the ground. "I told you, I don't want you doing this kind of work no more. It ain't good for the baby."

He kicked the iron jack out from under the wagon and left it lying in the yard, then returned his piqued eyes to his young wife, four months pregnant but still wearing blue jeans and loose cotton shirts under a thigh-length duck coat. Acquiring that soft, celestial look pregnant women get, Crystal grew more and more beautiful every day. But Jody tried hard not to let her looks soften his resolve on the matter at hand. He knew he was probably overreacting, but he couldn't help himself. He wanted nothing endangering the life of his unborn child and its mother.

"Oh, God, Jody! I can grease a wagon wheel! There's nothing to it!"

"The greasin' you can probably do," Jody allowed, "but you can't go manhandlin' a wagon jack!"

"I took it real slow. Besides, that axle had to be greased, and it sure as hell didn't look like you were going to do it. If you're going to make me drive around in this silly buggy until I deliver—which, I should add, is still five months away—I am not going to have its dang wheels creakin' so loud they're bustin' my eardrums!"

Jody regarded her tolerantly for several seconds, then set his mouth and shook his head, contrite. "All right, I should have greased the wheels when you told me they were squeakin'. I'm sorry. I guess I just thought you'd do what you usually do: harp at me until I had to do the job or leave the ranch."

Crystal allowed herself a thin smile as she grabbed Jody's coat and turned her head sideways to look up into the blue green eyes he'd inherited from his Irish father, "Milk River Bill" Harmon. "Sweety," she said, "getting pregnant doesn't turn women into glass. I'm not going to break like some china figurine. You have to let me do what I know I can do, or I'm going to go stark ravin' mad, sittin'

around all day on my thumbs!" She held his gaze
with hers.

Jody thought about it for a while. "Am I bein'
that bad?" he asked.

"Worse."

Jody shrugged. "Well . . . sorry. It's just"—he
turned his eyes to his father's grave under the cottonwood out by the creek—"it's just I lost Pa, you
know, and I don't know what I'd do if I lost you,
too. You and me, Crystal, we been together since
we were kids. . . ."

Crystal blinked tears back from her eyes as she
pressed her head against her husband's broad chest.
"You're not gonna lose me or the baby, Jody Harmon. Don't you worry about that. You aren't gonna
ever get rid of me . . . not until we're both ninety
years old and all our kids are grown and we're just
plum tired of each other."

"I'll never get tired of you, Crystal," Jody said,
wrapping her in his arms and sniffing her hair. "I
could never get tired of you."

Crystal squeezed her eyes shut and snuggled
deeper into Jody's chest, relishing the solid, mus-
cular feel of this man she'd known since they were
children riding horses together in the mountains . . .
neighboring ranch kids exploring caves and swim-
ming in creeks. She savored his musky, horsey
smell, wanting to curl up at his core.

But they both had work to do.

Finally, she lifted her smoky blue eyes to his and

said intimately, "You want lunch before you saddle another horse?"

Jody smiled. "Sure. You want me to fix it?"

Crystal gave a snort and stooped to retrieve her hat, which had blown against a wagon wheel. "Oh, I think your little china doll can fix lunch without breaking," she carped, then turned and headed for the cabin.

"Wait. Someone's comin'," Jody said.

Crystal turned to him, then followed his gaze out to the trail along the creek. About a half mile off, a rider appeared, cantering a black horse.

"Who's that?" Jody said.

"Beats me."

They both stood there and watched as the rider came through the cottonwoods, crossed the freshet leading to the creek, then passed through the Texas gate, scattering Crystal's chickens and attracting the collie pup who'd been feasting on something dead under the wagon.

The rider lifted an arm to wave, black hair bouncing around her shoulders and down her back.

"It's Fay," Jody said, then cast a curious look at Crystal.

Crystal shrugged. Fay Stillman often rode out to visit them on Saturdays. Before Crystal had started showing, she and Fay had ridden together in the mountains. They were best friends, having gotten acquainted back when Ben was investigating Fay's first husband's cattle rustling exploits and the murder of Jody's father. Crystal couldn't imagine what Fay was doing out here in the middle of the week, when school was on. She hoped nothing bad had happened to Mr. Stillman or Leon.

Uneasy, she walked out to meet the horse and rider. "Afternoon, Fay," she said, bending down to keep the deliriously happy pup from spooking the mare. "If I would have known you were coming, I would have stirred up some cookies and coffee cake."

"It was a spur of the moment decision," Fay said, climbing out of the leather as Jody held the mare's bridle.

"Oh?" Crystal asked. "Anything wrong?"

"Ben and I are both fine," Fay said, reading the concern in Crystal's eyes. She took Crystal's shoulders in her hands and appraised the pregnant young woman's condition. "You look lovely, and I do believe you're noticeably bigger than when I saw you in town last week."

"Bigger every day," Crystal groused. "I feel like a tick!"

She and Fay laughed.

Jody said, "Fay, I'll put your horse in the corral."

"Thanks, Jody."

Watching Jody lead the mare away, Crystal said, "No school today?"

Fay sighed, removed her hat, and slapped it

against her thigh, puffing dust. "I left early. That's why I'm here. Crystal, I need your help."

"Come on inside," Crystal said. "We'll discuss it over lunch."

9

OVER STEAMING BOWLS of stew and fresh bread, Fay told Crystal and Jody about her problem with Earl Hawley. While Jody was sympathetic, he couldn't come up with any clear solutions to the problem. It wasn't until after he'd bid Fay good luck, Crystal good-bye, and went out to the barn to saddle another horse, that Crystal told Fay what she thought they should do.

The women discussed it over another cup of coffee, ironing out the logistics. When Crystal saw Jody leave the yard on a gray gelding, she turned to Fay.

"Ready?"

"Crystal, are you sure?" Fay asked, standing with her back to the woodstove and holding a cup of coffee in her hands.

"Listen, I was raised by a drunk. I know what that little girl is going through."

"Well . . . that's why I wanted your advice," Fay mused.

"So, what are we waiting for?" Crystal said.

"This could be dangerous," Fay said. "And it's my problem. I should go alone."

"Not a chance," Crystal returned, opening the door.

Fay grabbed her hat. "At least drive the buggy."

"Not on your life."

"Crystal, Jody's going to think I'm a bad influence."

"You are." Crystal laughed. She stopped and turned to Fay. "Listen, I'll be home long before him, so he won't even know I left the ranch. Besides, if I don't get one last horseback ride between now and when the baby's born, I'm going to go nuts!" She gestured with her hands, then wheeled and headed for the barn.

Ten minutes later, the women were riding the wagon road northwest of the Harmon ranch, not saying much, an air of resolution in their bearing. Their long hair tumbled on their shoulders and blew in the breeze.

When they came to a valley sloping eastward, they turned their horses off the main trail and followed the shaggy wagon track between low ridges spiked with shrubs and Russian olives.

Fifteen minutes later, they topped a wooded hill overlooking the Hawley farm, which sat in a creek bottom, a cornfield peppered with crows flanking the small gray cabin, a log barn, and two sheds. A half dozen cows grazed in the pale-yellow corn and another two or three lounged along the creek. Chickens pecked in the yard and pigs milled in a pen behind the corral. The green wagon sat against the barn.

Fay brushed a lock of hair from her eyes and reconsidered her decision to come here and to involve Crystal. She should have waited and talked to Ben first. She should have . . .

"Let's go before we both start having second thoughts," Crystal said, pulling her horse around Fay's and heading down the hill toward the farmstead.

"Crystal," Fay called softly, wanting to call it off. But Crystal kept riding.

Fay sighed and touched Dorothy with her heels, descending the hill at a halfhearted walk. She and Crystal entered the farmyard riding stirrup to stirrup, looking around. Fay heard scraping sounds in the barn, but she saw no one in the yard. The hazy sun made everything look washed out and vaguely surreal. A cottonwood stood beside the house, and its fallen leaves blew this way and that, drifting against feed troughs and wagon wheels.

"Anyone home?" Crystal called.

Fay saw something move and turned to see a young girl in dirty overalls step through the open barn doors. Candace. She was carrying a pitchfork to which hay and dried manure clung. A short-haired, black and white mongrel with hanging teats appeared behind her. When it saw Fay and Crystal, it stormed their horses, barking.

"No, Missy, no!" Candace yelled at the dog.

When the dog saw that neither horse was going to bolt, only sidestep and crane their necks around curiously, it retreated behind Candace and growled, whimpering frustratedly.

"Hi, Candace," Fay said.

The little girl blinked her eyes. Her brown hair hung loose about her face, blowing in the wind. "Mrs.... *Stillman?*" she said, not quite believing her teacher was actually in her yard, straddling a horse!

"Are your parents home?"

As if to answer her question, a gruff male voice came from the house. "What in the hell is that goddamn dog barking about *now?*"

"I got her settled down now, Pa," Candace timidly replied.

Fay turned to the house, where Earl Hawley appeared, ambling onto the porch, a mean, angry look in his eyes. He wasn't wearing a hat, and his brown, gray-flecked hair was matted and mussed and standing in tufts. When he saw Fay and Crystal, he stopped and cocked his head as if for a better view. Fay guessed it wasn't every day a couple women on horseback entered his yard.

"What in the hell are you doing here?"

The man just stood there staring, rolling his eyes between Crystal and Fay, looking suspicious.

"Nice to see you again," Fay said, smiling and

cutting her eyes at Crystal, who smirked. "May we speak with you, Mr. Hawley?"

Hawley studied them for another couple seconds. Then a smile pulled at the corners of his mouth. "I see ya brought a little muscle." He laughed.

Crystal looked at Fay.

Fay said, "This is your neighbor, Crystal Harmon. She just came along for the ride."

"I bet she did."

Mrs. Hawley appeared in the door, behind her husband. There was a cut on her cheek, just under her right eye, and another on her chin.

"Hello, Noreen," Crystal said. "We came to talk to you and Earl about getting Candace back in school."

Noreen Hawley looked as though she'd had the life wrung out of her. She was a frightened, lonely woman, with the haunted look of an animal on the run from something much larger and more relentless than she. She glanced at her husband. "I—I don't think we better . . . I don't think so, Crystal." Fay could barely hear her.

"Please let us come inside, ma'am," Fay said.

"You better not," Mrs. Hawley said.

"Your men know where you're at?" Hawley asked. He smiled that lewd leer Fay had seen when he and Candace were leaving the school.

She and Crystal shared another meaningful glance. Then Fay said, "We're here of our own accord, Mr. Hawley."

Hawley's hooded eyes were mean and calculating. Thoughts were at work behind them, Fay could tell. Lecherous thoughts. The man's cold, wanton expression sprouted goose bumps along her spine.

He stepped aside and grinned. "Well, come on in," he said, brandishing an arm at the open doorway where his wife stood, huddled up against the jamb, her face blanched with fear.

Fay looked at Crystal apprehensively. She turned and saw Candace watching from the barn, looking small and unhappy and lonely, completely powerless to better her life, utterly dependent upon others . . . like Fay.

Turning back to Crystal, Fay said, "You can stay here with the horses."

"No," Crystal said, dismounting.

They tied their horses at the hitchrack before the porch and mounted the steps. Fay looked at Hawley standing there, grinning, his big cruel face puffy from alcohol, his breath sweet with the smell of homemade wine.

Feeling uneasy, she walked past him and went inside, where Mrs. Hawley fidgeted around the stove, wringing her hands and looking about the small, cluttered kitchen as if for a place to hide. Probably feeling ashamed of the filth, the broken chairs and table, the empty whiskey bottles lying on the floor by the stove. The place smelled like rotten food, slop pails, sweat, and alcohol. Fay thought of Candace, trapped here with this animal, her father, and felt so enraged she feared she'd cry.

Hawley filled the doorway, grinning, having a good time. "Well, what do you say we all sit down and have a drink?"

"We didn't come here to drink with you, Mr. Hawley. We came here to talk with you about Candace."

Hawley walked over to the rocker by the woodstove and retrieved a crock jug. He brought the jug to the table, uncorked it, and set it down. Scarlet liquid sloshed over the lip.

"Noreen, bring us some glasses."

Hawley looked dully at his wife, who made no move to obey him. He scowled.

"You know what, ladies?" he said to Fay and Crystal. "My wife here doesn't approve of my drinking." His features formed a mock serious expression, regarding Fay and Crystal each in turn, as if they had a perplexing problem on their hands.

Then, suddenly, before either woman knew what was happening, the man made a dash for his wife, grabbing her by an arm and the back of her neck, and led her out the cabin door, screaming.

Fay froze, stunned. She managed to move to the door in time to see the cursing, red-faced Hawley throw his wife off the porch. The woman hit the ground on wobbly legs and fell on her butt with a startled grunt, head lolling on her shoulders.

"That's what I do to spoilsports, Noreen," Hawley yelled from the porch. "Simple as that. You can just stay out there while me and these pretty young gals have us a party inside."

Fay looked around Hawley at his wife. Dumbfounded, the woman sat in the dirt, legs spread out before her. As her mind caught up to what had just happened, her face crumpled with embarrassment and horror and pain, and she sagged sideways, her mouth opening with a silent scream. Head between her arms, face in the dirt, she whimpered like a child.

Her heart breaking for the poor woman, Fay started toward her. Hawley turned in her path, his six-foot bulk blocking the steps.

"Done got rid of the ol' spoilsport," he said, very pleased with himself.

Grinning, he moved toward Fay, who swallowed and took three involuntary steps backward into the cabin, her heart pounding against her breastbone. She wondered vaguely where Crystal was, not wanting to take her eyes off the dangerous Hawley long enough to look around. Then she backed into her friend, and the two of them stood there, regarding the ominous Earl Hawley attentively.

"Momma!" Candace cried from the barn. Behind Hawley, Fay saw the little girl run to her mother.

Inside the cabin, Hawley kicked the door closed and regarded Fay and Crystal lustily. "Now which one of you wants to go first?" he said, lowering his hands to his crotch and unbuttoning the fly of his torn, greasy denims.

"I do, Mr. Hawley," Crystal said.

She took two steps toward him, carrying something. She brought up the two-by-four with both hands and, with a vigorous grunt, heaved it forward into Hawley's chest. Hawley gave a startled cry and fell back against the door with an astonished expression on his face.

"Hey . . . what . . . *wait!*"

"You wait, you sick son of a bitch," Crystal groused through gritted teeth.

She raised the two-by-four above her shoulder and brought it down through Hawley's upraised hands to his skull with a satisfying smack. He hit the floor on his butt, stared for a few seconds until his eyes dimmed and rolled back in his head. Then he fell sideways and lay still.

Fay stood there, staring at the man. After several seconds, she swung her gaze to Crystal, standing over the unconscious Hawley, breathing heavily, the two-by-four hanging at her side. Neither woman could quite work her mind around what had just occurred.

Finally Fay said, looking at the board in Crystal's right hand, "Where did you get that?"

"Behind the door," Crystal said, catching her breath.

"Is he . . . is he dead?" Fay said, taking a tentative step toward Hawley.

Crystal went down on a knee, inspecting the man from a distance, half-expecting him to suddenly reach out and grab her. "No, he's breathing," Crystal said.

There was another uneasy silence.

"Well, that was a bust," Fay said nervously.

Still on her knees, Crystal turned to her. "It doesn't have to be."

"What?"

"I think it's time ol' Earl took the cure, don't you?"

Fay shook her head slightly, frowning. "What . . . what are you saying?"

"I say we lock the son of a bitch in his barn for a few days, let him dry out. Maybe once all that alcohol's out of his system, he'll be a little easier to deal with."

"What about his wife? What about Candace?" Fay knew that even if they locked the man in his barn, his wife would probably succumb to his screaming and let him out. He'd cowed her well. Then he'd probably kill both her and his daughter.

"They could come over and live with me and Jody for a couple weeks. Or you could take them to town. Jody and I'll tend the stock while Earl's dryin' out."

Fay took a deep breath and turned in a circle, wringing her hands together. "Crystal, this is crazy."

"No, *this* is crazy," Crystal said, returning her gaze to Hawley. "He's crazy like my father. What he did to me and my ma and my brothers and sisters, this man is doing to his family. I say we lock the son of a bitch in the barn until he dries out. If it doesn't change him, if he doesn't stay dried out, then we find another home for Mrs. Hawley and Candace." She looked at Fay and shook her head. "They can't stay here."

Fay looked into her friend's eyes, where the hurt of her childhood was almost palpable. Crystal's father had killed Jody's father in a drunken rage, because Warren Johnson had not wanted his daughter marrying a half-breed. That was in her eyes now, along with sixteen years of abuse. She knew such horror from the inside, and her resolute gaze told Fay she would not, could not, let it continue here.

"They can stay with Ben and me," Fay said. "That way Candace can attend school."

They found Mrs. Hawley sitting in a chair on the porch. She was holding Candace in her lap. They'd both been crying.

Mrs. Hawley looked at them worriedly. "What . . . what's happened?" she said.

Candace was straddling her mother's knee, lying back against the woman's bosom, her head under Mrs. Hawley's chin. Her eyes were open and staring. She did not react to either Fay or Crystal.

"I conked him on the head with a two-by-four," Crystal said. "He's out, but he won't be out long."

Fay knelt before Mrs. Hawley and gazed up into the woman's sad, muddy, tear-streaked face. "Here's what we want to do," she said, and told her the plan.

Mrs. Hawley cried, her head in her hands, as
though she were more afraid of change than of her
drunken husband. Finally, though, after letting her
tear-filled eyes stray across the barnyard unseeingly,
taking stock of her life, considering the bleak future
if things remained as they were—if *he* remained as
he was—she turned to Fay and Crystal and nodded
her head.

"Why don't you and Candace go inside and
pack?" Fay said. "Crystal and I will get your husband out to the barn."

Getting a two-hundred-pound man bound and
dragged off the porch and into the barn wasn't an
easy task, but they managed it with the help of one
of their horses, their nerves stretched thin with the
need to hurry. If Hawley woke up, he'd require another blow to the head, which could kill him.

When he was bound with ropes and chain and
secured to a horse stall, they set out two heavy horse
blankets and a pan of water, brushed the dirt and
hay from their sweaty clothes, and headed outside,
where Mrs. Hawley and Candace waited in the green
wagon. The black and white mongrel was standing
on its hind legs, nuzzling Candace, who patted it
absently.

"The dog will be fine," Crystal said. "Me and
Jody will feed her and your milch cow." Turning to
Mrs. Hawley, who wore fresh clothes and a straw
hat but whose face was still puffy with tears, she
said, "We'll both look after Earl. When he's ready,

we'll tell him where you are, so he can come for you . . . if you want him to."

The woman nodded stiffly and turned to Crystal. She didn't say anything, but a very thin smile pulled at her lips.

10

LEON MCMANNIGLE RODE back to Clantick facing a strong northwesterly wind that flattened his hat brim against his forehead and made him squint his eyes against dust blowing up from the road ahead of him. He went directly to the jail to see if anyone was waiting for him and Ben with an emergency to report, or to see if anyone had scribbled a message on the note Ben had left on the door.

Finding nothing at the jail, he checked with Sam Wa and Evelyn, who kept an unofficial eye on the jail when Ben and Leon weren't there. All had been quiet while the lawmen were away, Evelyn reported.

"Well, in that case, I reckon I'll have a bite to eat," he said, tossing his hat on the counter and sliding onto a stool, eyeing the sugarcoated donuts in a glass-covered display pan. "I sure am hungry."

"Well, what happened out to the Hagen farm?" Evelyn asked him.

She stood behind the counter, one hand on her hip, the other holding a coffeepot. Sam Wa stood in the doorway leading back to the kitchen, looking at Leon expectantly. They'd both been waiting to hear, as was probably half the town by now. News traveled fast, especially when three-quarters of Clantick's population passed through Sam Wa's every day, to hear it from Evelyn. Since she had a bird's-eye view of the jail across the street, she'd become the county's unofficial herald.

Leon knew from the way Evelyn was holding the coffeepot and Sam was holding fast to his position in the kitchen doorway, that he wasn't going to get so much as a splash of coffee until he'd told them everything. So that's what he did.

Not that there was much to tell. Hansel Hagen had been murdered, it appeared, by the same person who'd murdered the mulatto. The motive for the killings of two such disparate citizens was anyone's guess, and no doubt everyone in town would soon be guessing. Sam Wa's would be hopping for supper tonight, as everyone came in for the news from Evelyn and Sam.

"That's just awful," Evelyn whispered, bringing a hand to her mouth.

"Yes, it is," Leon said, his eyes returning to the donuts. "Now, could I get lunch and about six of those goldang donuts?"

"Coming right up," Sam Wa said and disappeared into the kitchen.

Evelyn finally turned over a cup and was filling it when she stopped suddenly, spilling coffee, to stare out the window. "Someone's lookin' for you," she told Leon.

The deputy turned on his stool to follow her gaze to the jail, where a slight man in a tattered suit was pounding on the door. He'd already turned and started for the café when Leon opened Wa's door and stepped onto the boardwalk, wondering if he was doomed to miss lunch and his sugar-covered donuts.

"What do you have, Hyram?" Leon asked the man, a shell-shocked Civil War veteran who delivered newspapers for Evan Danielson, the young Easterner who wrote and printed the weekly Clantick *Courant*.

Hyram Pyle stepped up on the boardwalk, a load of freshly printed papers under his arm. "I—I seen someone jump off the roof of the Miller place."

The Miller place was a big Victorian house built by Frederick Miller, who owned the lumber yards in both Clantick and Chinook and was in the process of establishing another in Big Sandy. The Hi-Line's building boom in recent years had made the man wealthy beyond his Prussian immigrant's wildest dreams.

"Someone working on the house?" Leon asked Hyram Pyle.

Pyle squinted his milky blue eyes, his hollow, unshaven cheeks flushed with drama. "He jumped down off'n that roof and ran like a bat outta hell, like he was up to no good, sure 'nough!"

"All right, I'll take a look at it, Hyram. Thanks." He tossed the deliveryman a nickel and told him to have some coffee and sugar donuts on him, and jogged across the street, where his horse was tethered to the hitchrack before the jailhouse.

Leon trotted his horse east down First Street, then hung a right down Second Avenue, heading south. He'd gone about fifty yards when he turned his head to look behind a row of white frame houses, smoke from their chimneys tearing in the wind, and froze in the saddle, bringing his horse to a halt.

There, amid piles of stacked cordwood, trash heaps, and privies, a man in a dark coat and hat was walking toward Leon, head turned to the side. When the head turned forward, the man saw Leon and stopped dead in his tracks.

Leon frowned, feeling a shot of adrenaline squirt in his veins. He didn't know why, but something told him this was the one . . . this was the man who'd killed Cadena and Hansel Hagen. His heart picked up, and his breath grew short.

Then the man turned sharply to his right and fled, disappearing behind a house.

Cursing, Leon reined his horse down the alley. "Come on, horse, gidup! *Go!*"

He turned his horse around the house, following the killer's path, and reined to a sudden halt. Finding himself in the backyard of another shack, with a line of clothes drying in the cool wind, he looked around, seeing no sign of the man who had fled. Shacks, shanties, and privies lay willy-nilly around him, smoke puffing from their chimneys and scenting the air with cottonwood and pine. Then he heard a dog barking over the hill to his left, and he spurred his horse that way.

On the other side of the hill he cast his gaze toward Auld's Livery Barn, where horses were running in the paddock that spilled down the grade behind the white frame barn. Something or someone had spooked them.

Heart racing, Leon spurred his black toward the paddock, dismounted, not bothering to tie the reins, and ducked through the rails into the corral. The spooked horses eyed him warily and jerked their heads over the opposite fence.

"Shh . . . easy, easy now," he whispered to Auld's saddle stock, moving through them with his revolver drawn, heading for the open barn doors.

Just inside the door, he stopped to listen and look around. Two big Percherons stood in a nearby stall, craning their heads around to see Leon. The wariness in their eyes told the deputy he wasn't the only intruder here.

The hair pricked on the back of his neck as he turned right and headed down the wide alley, through the rich barn smells, between stalls of tethered stock and wagons for rent, feeling cobwebs brush his face. The shadows engulfed him, making him feel vulnerable and alone. A man could easily hide in such shadows, wait for Leon to pass, then come up behind him with a knife.

The possibility jerked him around to cover his back. Nothing but the alley and parked wagons and the open barn doors about fifty feet away and to the right ... the milling horses and tools hanging on joists and walls ... the summer's last flies droning against the windows.

Then he heard a foot come down in the hay and grit behind him.

His heart leaped as he wheeled, swinging the Remington. But before he could make out the dark-clad figure before him, something heavy slammed into his head, spinning him around and down, his ears screaming, skull exploding with pain.

He only vaguely heard the bark of his revolver before he was on the floor and tumbling rapidly through warm, black, liquid unconsciousness.

Stillman rode into town two hours later, as the sun was setting behind the brown, chalky buttes west of Clantick. His face was burned raw from the sun and wind, and his butt was blistered.

He was tired, both physically and emotionally. There was nothing more frustrating or draining than tracking a crafty killer—especially one preying on the very citizens you've been paid to protect, and who've entrusted you with their protection.

But try as he might to find the killer, spending

half the day in the country around the Hagen farm, he'd discovered nothing. Not a single clue. The man hadn't left one hoofprint near the Hagen barn, so the hour and a half Stillman had spent trying to cut the man's trail had proven as fruitful as tracking a bird in flight.

His conversation with Hagen's widow hadn't turned anything up, either. All the hysterical young Kirsti could tell him was that she'd fallen asleep last night before her husband had returned from his nightly visit to the barn. When she woke in the morning and found that his side of the bed hadn't been slept in, she went out to the barn and found him pitchforked to the inside of the barn door.

Tethering his horse to the hitchrack before the jailhouse, Stillman winced at the image of the poor woman—only twenty-five years old, with three kids and another on the way—crying hysterically over the gruesome death of her young husband. What would she do now? Where would she go? How would she and her children live?

The whole dilemma made his heart sick and his chest ache as he moved to the jailhouse door and turned the knob with a sigh. It was locked. Only then did Stillman glance at the window upon which Hill County Sheriff had been painted in a gold-leaf arc. No light, either. Which meant Leon must be on his rounds.

He stuck his hand in his jeans pocket to fish for the

door key. Just as he grabbed it he heard, "Sheriff . . . oh, Sheriff Stillman . . ."

Stillman turned to see Evelyn Vincent jogging across the street from Sam Wa's.

"It's Leon. . . . He's been hurt," the waitress said as she reached the hitchrack before the jail, clutching a shawl around her shoulders.

Stillman's pulse quickened. He frowned. "Where is he?"

Evelyn jerked a thumb westward. "At Doc Evans's. Someone hit him in the head in Auld's Livery Barn."

Stillman reached for his reins. "Who?" he demanded.

Evelyn shook her head. "We don't know. He's unconscious, and whoever it was ran away." She watched Stillman worriedly as he climbed into the leather. "I hope . . . I hope he's all right. Please let me know, will you, how he is?"

"Will do, Evelyn . . . and thanks," Stillman said, grimly kicking his horse westward down First.

He knew Sweets was tired from the all-day ride, but Stillman's concern for his deputy made him spur the horse into a gallop up the butte at the edge of town. Sitting atop the butte were the doctor's red frame house, privy, and stable, all looking customarily shabby. This was where the doctor, who doubled as an undertaker, plied his trade, but Evans cared little for appearances. His belief was that, since he was the only doctor and undertaker in town,

he could work out of a cattle car and see no dimi-
nution of business whatsoever, and Stillman thought
the arrogant bastard was probably right.

Stillman dismounted his horse, tied him to the
hitchrack, and mounted the porch. He knocked on
the door and went in, crossing the foyer to the
kitchen, which did double duty as the doctor's office. Evans was there, working at the table with a
mortar and pestle. He did not look up as Stillman
entered.

"He's in there," Evans said, jerking his head at a
door opening off the kitchen. "You can have a look,
but he's dead out."

Stillman opened the door and glanced in the
room. Leon lay in bed, mounded with blankets and
quilts. A thick white bandage had been wrapped
around his head. His eyes were squeezed painfully
closed.

Stillman shut the door and turned to the doctor,
still working at the table with his sleeves rolled up
to his elbows. There was a fire in the stove, and the
kitchen smelled like coffee and medicine.

"What happened?"

"Someone hit him with a singletree in Auld's Livery. Most singletrees are made of oak or hickory.
They don't give much when they're brought in con-
tact with the human skull."

"Who did it—anyone see?"

"No, but Auld walked in just as the man was
about to cut Leon's throat. Auld even took a shot at

him, but his buckshot missed as the man fled through the paddock. Big man, Auld said. Wearing a dark coat and hat. Didn't see his face." Evans turned to Stillman. "Our killer?"

"Must be. How in the hell did Leon corner him in the livery barn?"

Evans shrugged. "I guess Hyram Pyle reported someone jumping from the second story of the Miller place. Leon must have ridden over to check it out, ran into the killer, and chased him into the barn." Evans shook his head. "The man did fast work over at Miller's."

Stillman's stomach did a flip. "What do you mean?"

"Miller's wife came home and found Miller's elderly mother dead in her upstairs room." Again, Evans looked up from his work. "Her throat had been cut. I went over and checked it out. Same type of cut we found on the bodies of Cadena and the drummer."

Stillman's thoughts had lagged behind the doctor's story. He removed his hat, sat across from the doctor, and put his hand on the man's wrist. "Wait a minute. You're saying there's been another murder?"

"Just said so, didn't I?"

"Frederick Miller's mother?"

"That's what I said." Evans pulled his wrist out of Stillman's grasp and continued working, grinding what looked like herbs in the mortar.

"Holy smokes," Stillman said, running his open hand through the thick, salt-and-pepper hair curling over his ears. "Where were Mr. and Mrs. Miller?"

"Miller was at work. His wife was having tea across town with the mayor's wife." The doctor shook his head. "They told me they wanted to see you as soon as you returned from the country. They're not happy. Not a bit."

"No . . . I reckon not," Stillman said with a sigh.

"Oh, I don't think either one of them is sorry to see the old lady go—she was as cantankerous a Prussian peasant wench as you'll find in the Western world—but the idea of their home being invaded and one of their family hacked up like a jack-o'-lantern has them bristling, to say the least." Evans chuckled.

Stillman regarded the man dully and shook his head. Leave it to Evans to find humor in the least humorous of situations. "How's Leon doing?" the sheriff asked.

Evans shrugged, set down the pestle, and sat back in his chair. He looked tired but sober, for which Stillman felt fortunate. He'd seen the man do some of his best work inebriated, but he wanted him sober when he was working on Leon.

"Fractured skull," Evans said. "Not real bad, but not good, either. Concussion. I suspect he'll be out for a few hours, but he'll come out of it . . . with one hell of a headache."

Stillman indicated the mortar bowl. "What's that?"

"I'm grinding willow bark and cayenne pepper to make a tea. I'm going to give it to Leon when he comes around. In his condition, I think it's best he stay away from laudanum or morphine."

Stillman nodded thoughtfully, feeling almost too tired to work his mind over the problem that seemed to grow by the second.

"You still think it was me?" Evans asked, looking at Stillman bemusedly.

Stillman met his gaze. He was grateful to be able to write the doctor off his suspect list, short as it was. In spite of the man's sardonic wit, Stillman felt an affinity with him, a vague camaraderie. The doctor was more like Stillman than Stillman cared to admit.

He shook his head. "You're looking doubtful."

"Who do you think?"

"I haven't the foggiest idea. You have any suspicions?"

Evans shook his head and cast his gaze at the herbs in the bowl. "Nope. I usually have a sense about these things, but the only sense I have now is that this guy is going to do it again. Soon."

"Why?" Stillman said forcefully, his big face flushing with anger. "There's got to be a reason why he's killing these people. What is it?"

Evans shrugged and got up to grab a log from the wood box. "Maybe he likes it."

Stillman pondered it. Nodding thoughtfully, he said, "No, there's a pattern here. All four victims are too unrelated for there not to be some hidden pattern or method to the bastard's madness. Something relates his victims in some way. *Something.*"

"What could Fredericka Miller and Cadena Martin possibly have in common?" Evans asked as he tossed the log through the stove's open door.

Stillman looked at the doctor, but his mind was on the question. Finally his face fell and he shook his head in defeat.

"I don't know." He grabbed his hat off the table and put it on as he headed for the door. "Keep me posted on Leon, will you? I'm going to the Millers' now, but I'll be back at the jail in about an hour. I'll be spending the night there, it looks like. There and making the rounds."

"Sort of like a collie dog guarding the sheep, eh?" Evans called.

"More like a poodle," Stillman groused and slammed the door behind him.

11

STILLMAN WENT OVER to the big Miller house and found a half-dozen horse-drawn rigs pulled up at the picket fence, blue moonlight reflecting off the polished leather seats. His clapper knock was answered by a hired girl in a dusting cap. She led him down the main hall, past a parlor filled with well-dressed women and the smell of conflicting perfumes, to a closed door under the stairs.

Before he turned through the door the girl had opened after a single knock, he glanced through the door opening to his right and glimpsed a naked, white-haired body spread out on a long kitchen table. The body was so white it resembled a bleached prune. Two girls stood around the table, cleaning the body with sponges dipped in water bowls. Their eyes met Stillman's sheepishly. Neither appeared to have much stomach for their current assignment.

"Sheriff Stillman is here, Mr. Miller," the girl before Stillman announced to the study, where five

men in dark suits and waistcoats sat on wing chairs
and on a couch against a wall.

A fire crackled in the hearth, mixing the smell of
pine with the rich smell of expensive cigars. Raking
his eyes over the six men in the room, Stillman recognized the mayor and four members of the city
council, in addition to Frederick Miller. The Prussian immigrant who'd only recently made his modest fortune in the lumber business stood puffing a
silver-rimmed pipe before the fire. He must have
called in the city council when he'd learned his
mother had been killed, the sheriff's deputy was comatose, and Stillman was nowhere to be found.

"Sheriff," the lean, dark man announced in his
heavy Prussian accent, "it is about time you arrive!"

The girl glanced at Stillman, her features coloring,
and drifted back out to the hall, swinging the door
closed behind her.

"I'm very sorry, Mr. Miller, about the trouble
you've seen here today," Stillman said, turning his
ten-gallon hat in his hands. Situations like this always made him feel like a bull in a dining room.

Miller strode to him jerkily, angry and agitated,
his clean-scrubbed face reflecting the fire's buttery
glow. "Some man entered my house and killed my
mother!" the man fairly yelled, breathing heavily.
"Cut her throat!"

"So I'm told. I want to offer my personal con-
dolences and assure you that I'm going to do everything in my power to find the killer." Stillman knew

how hollow his words sounded, but what the hell else was he supposed to say? Times like this he wished he had stayed at his Pinkerton desk job in Denver. Or remained retired.

"I thought you'd cleaned up the town," Miller said accusingly.

"Yes . . ." Stillman said with a sigh. "I thought so, too."

One of the other men, Rolf Garrity, president of the town council and owner of Garrity's Feed Store, cleared his throat. "Ben, do you have any idea who might have killed Mrs. Miller?"

Stillman turned to him sharply, angry that it had taken the death of a prominent man's mother to arouse the interest of the city council. No use reminding them of that now. They'd only use it against him. Four people dead in less than three days, and he didn't have one single clue as to who was doing the killing.

Stillman stifled his anger and said simply, "No."

Edgar Tempe, the barber who moonlighted as mayor, squirmed in the wing chair before the desk. "This is intolerable, Sheriff," he said. "This is supposed to be a civilized town. If word gets out that we have a killer on the loose, people are going to stop coming to town. They're going to stop shopping here. They're going to drive over to Chinook or Big Sandy!" He looked at the other men for concurrence.

Dwight Utley, an attorney, agreed. "Just today I

had a man say he thought Clantick was safer back when Bernard McFadden's men were shooting up First Street. At least you knew who was doing the killing!"

"When this gets out," the mercantile owner, Leroy Pepin, said, puffing his stogey, his small blue eyes looking fishy behind the thick lenses of his pince-nez glasses, "business is going to fall off sharply. We'll all see it in our accounts next week." He gave a self-satisfied grunt and a nod and went back to work on the stogey.

"I'm damn scared for my wife and kids, Ben!" Rolf Garrity said.

The others loudly agreed, nodding their heads and glancing at each other like a roomful of fat, super-cilious monarchs suddenly facing the prospect of barbarians storming their white picket fences.

"All right, all right, all right," Stillman said, hold-ing up both hands for quiet as he made his way to a chair. "Settle down and take a deep breath. Pan-icking will get us nowhere fast." He sat down, hik-ing a boot on his knee. He surveyed his suddenly quiet audience, watching him now like befuddled students.

"This is a bad situation, probably as bad as I've seen, but if you all get snakes in your shorts and go around making the rest of the town nervous, it's only going to get worse." He paused for emphasis. "This guy isn't just some drifter comin' through. I think he's one of us. Hell, he could be one of you sitting before me."

This set up a clamor as the men looked around at each other, looking insulted.

"This is insanity!" Miller fumed, glaring at Stillman. "A man comes into my own house and kills my mother, and you're telling me I could be the killer!"

Stillman raised his hand again. "All right, pipe *down*," Stillman carped, feeling more and more fatigued. "I didn't say it *was* one of you, just that it's definitely someone in town. And since most of you have lived here longer than I have, I'm going to need your help in finding him."

Miller stomped his foot in exasperation. "Isn't that what we hired you for?"

Stillman's fatigued eyes rose to the lumberman's with an extreme air of overstressed tolerance. "Miller, set your ass down," he ordered.

The room was so silent you could hear the fire sucking air. Someone broke wind.

Miller looked around as if for help. Getting none, he sank slowly back in his chair, eyes returning to Stillman.

"Good 'nough," the sheriff said. "Now, the job my deputy and I have ahead of us is a tough one. It's also one that neither of us has done before. So we're going to need nothing but your unwavering support and assistance. If by Saturday we haven't caught the son of a bitch who killed Miller's mother here—as well as Cadena Martin, Mr. Dawson, and Hansel Hagen—then I'll turn in my badge and try to find someone else who can."

Again, he paused for emphasis. The expressions facing him had transformed from red-faced indignation to dubious interest.

Stillman continued. "But I don't think that's going to be necessary. I think that once I find out what this man's motivation is, I'll have him. But first I need to learn why he's targeted these four people. Which leads me to the question I have for each of you. What do these four have in common?"

They thought about it, glancing at each other puzzledly.

Miller said with a scoff, "What could that . . . *whore* . . . have possibly had in common with my mother?"

Stillman turned to him impassively. "That's what I'm askin' you."

"Well, I never," Miller said, rolling his eyes.

"Think about it, Miller," Stillman urged him. "What could your mother, Cadena Martin, and Hansel Hagen have had in common?"

"Nothing!"

Stillman turned to the others. "What about the rest of you? What event could tie the mulatto with Hagen?"

"Maybe he visited her on occasion," Garrity said sheepishly, apparently reluctant to suggest his own connection to the whore. Stillman knew that most if not all the men present in this room had probably taken carnal pleasure in the mulatto's humble cabin.

"But I doubt Miller's mother did," Stillman said, straight-faced.

The mayor snickered and Miller cowed him with a look.

"This is ridiculous," Miller said to Stillman. "My mother had no connection with that whore or that farmer . . . Hansel . . . whatever his name . . ."

"What about the drummer?" Tempe asked Stillman from behind a thick, blue cloud of cigar smoke.

"I'm thinking he was just an unlucky bystander, Mayor," Stillman said. "Unless any of you can tell me otherwise."

None of them could.

After a long, thoughtful silence, Stillman donned his hat and said, "Well, you'll know where to find me if you come up with anything. If you'll excuse me, I'd like to go upstairs and have a look at the room your mother was killed in, Mr. Miller."

Miller nodded grudgingly and spat in the fire. "It's the second one to the left, on the second story."

Stillman started for the door and stopped, remembering another question he had for Miller. "Was your front door unlocked this afternoon?"

Miller nodded. "It's always open," he groused.

"Why did the killer leave by the roof?"

"He must have heard the hired girl arrive. She always arrives at two."

"Much obliged," Stillman said.

He closed the door behind him, walked down the hall, and turned up the stairs. He stopped at the door Miller had indicated and turned the knob.

He fumbled in the dark for a lantern. When he got it lit, he inspected the room—as large a bedroom as Stillman had ever seen, with a four-door armoire, a walk-in closet, and an oak four-poster bed. The bed had been stripped, but blood remained on the mattress—a great inky smudge that would never come out, no matter how long one of the hired girls scrubbed at it.

Stillman turned to one of the three windows and raised the lantern. The yellow light fell on the porch roof just below the window. The killer, hearing the hired girl, had gone out the window, onto the roof, and jumped from the roof to the ground. Not long after, he'd run into Leon.

"Crafty son of a bitch," Stillman carped aloud, staring at the light on the porch roof. Nimble one, too, he thought, to have jumped that far without breaking an ankle or leg.

Stillman lifted his gaze, looking north toward First Street, where lights glowed faintly behind the false fronts of the business district. The rest of the town was dark but where the moon reflected off a house or privy.

Stillman stood staring out the window for a long

time, his mind working over the possibilities, all the faces he'd seen, all the people he'd come to know, realizing that one of them was a killer.

Knowing that somewhere out there . . . or in this very house . . . he lurked.

Knowing he'd strike again . . .

12

STILLMAN LEFT THE Miller house and walked Sweets directly to the stable behind the jailhouse. As he unsaddled the bay, he noticed the right rear shoe was again loose and made a mental note to have it reset. There was no hurry, however. After all the ground he'd covered today, the horse needed a break. Tomorrow Stillman would rent another mount from Auld at the livery barn.

When he'd rubbed down the horse with a burlap scrap and fed and watered him, he went into the jailhouse, got a fire going in the woodstove, then checked to make sure his Henry rifle was loaded and ready to go. That done, he loaded the three spare Winchesters chained and padlocked in the rack across from his desk.

He wasn't sure why he needed all four rifles loaded. He suspected he merely needed to occupy his hands while he tried to come up with a link between all four of the killer's victims. Something told him that once he knew that link, he'd not only know who the next victim would be, he'd have his killer.

But would he be able to come up with that link before the killer struck again?

He twisted a cigarette and sat in his desk chair, smoking and listening to the stove tick as it heated, racking his brain to come up with any possible link between a whore, a drummer, a farmer, and an old lady from Prussia. What in hell could four such different people have in common?

"Well, this isn't getting me anywhere," he told himself, craning his neck to glance at the clock. Six-thirty. Fay would be wondering where he was.

He got up and banked the fire, adding his cigarette stub to the conflagration. He'd go home and let Fay know what was happening. Then he'd return to the jail to restoke the fire—the jailhouse would be his base of operations for the night—and start walking the streets. Without knowing who the next victim would be, the only thing he could do to keep the town safe was to make his presence known, minute by minute, hour by hour, all night long. All tomorrow, too, if need be.

The town didn't cover much over a half square mile, and Stillman thought he could cover it pretty thoroughly even without Leon's help. Covering it alone would be exhausting, but he'd return to the jail every couple of hours for a catnap and coffee before heading out again.

He couldn't cover the whole county, but he had to cover something. He couldn't just go home and crawl into bed and wait for the bastard to strike again. Leon should be well enough to help in a few days. Stillman could last that long. He had to.

Walking home in the chill autumn twilight, he noted the town looked different than it normally did at this hour. There were still the ponies tethered before the saloons and brothels and the obligatory ranch wagon parked before Hall's Mercantile, but the atmosphere was somehow restrained. Most of the windows along First Street were dark, and those that cast their lantern light on the boardwalks and street did so weakly, with a tentative air. Stillman wasn't sure if it was the time of the year, the early sunset, the wind, or just his imagination. But the town looked eerie . . . like you'd expect a town to look, haunted by a madman.

Stillman turned his collar up against the chill, cut through an alley to French Street, and opened the gate in the picket fence. He threw the door open and was met by a scream. Startled, he swung his gaze to a little brown-haired girl reading a book on the davenport against the living room's east wall, under the big elk head that had come with the house. The girl watched him with wide-eyed fear.

Fay and another woman came running from the kitchen. Glancing from Ben to the girl, Fay stopped as the other woman moved past her to the girl. Fay looked at Stillman. "I was wondering where you've been. I was worried."

"I didn't mean to frighten the child," Stillman said, watching the woman comfort the girl, who sobbed once over her mother's shoulder, turning a wary brown eye back to Stillman.

"It's all right, Candace," Fay said, moving to the girl. "This is my husband, Ben. He's the sheriff here in Clantick. He's here to protect us."

Stillman quelled the urge to laugh. Lately he felt about as capable of protection as this child, but he smiled and gave the girl a wink. "That's right, honey." He folded his coat back to reveal his sheriff's badge. "See my star?"

Stillman had always been amazed at the ability of two bits' worth of tin to lend comfort and inspire optimism—in children as well as adults. It was one of the main things he'd always liked about pinning it to his shirt. It wasn't always easy, however—during times like these—to stand behind it.

The girl's face acquired some color and her eyes lost their fear. The woman turned to him shyly and straightened, pressing her dress smooth against her legs.

"Ben, this is Mrs. Hawley and her daughter, Candace," Fay said. "They're going to spend a couple of days with us."

"If . . . if that's all right with you, of course, Mr. Stillman," Mrs. Hawley hurried to add, keeping her chin low, as though it were a physical effort to lift it. Stillman suspected it had something to do with the bruises on her face, bruises Stillman knew from experience could only have been put there by a man. Suddenly he thought he understood the girl's initial fear of him.

"Any guest of my lovely wife's is a guest of mine," Stillman said, remembering his hat and quickly removing it, striding over to the woman and shaking her hand. "Pleased to meet you, Mrs. Hawley." He turned his smile to the girl. "And you, too, Candace. You like horses?"

The corner of the child's mouth lifted slightly. She nodded.

"Well, I've got a fine one I'd like you to see. His name's Sweets. He's over at the jailhouse stable now, but I'll bring him over here soon, and you can ride him. How would that be?"

The girl's brightening eyes slid from Stillman to her mother then back to Stillman, and she gave her shoulder a shrug.

"It's a date, then," Stillman said, hoping he'd be able to find time for the girl, who obviously needed some cheering up. "Now, if you ladies will excuse me, I have to change my rather ripe-smelling shirt and get back to work."

He looked at Fay meaningfully, then disappeared down the hall to their bedroom. A moment later, Fay followed him in, closing the door behind her and frowning.

"What's happened?" she asked.

"He's struck again. Killed Mrs. Miller and knocked Leon unconscious."

"Oh, my God," Fay gasped. "That poor woman . . . and . . . is Leon all right?"

Stillman was removing his shirt. "Doc thinks so."

Fay took the dirty shirt from Stillman, tossed it on the laundry pile, and went to the dresser for a fresh one. "Where . . . how did it happen?" she asked, her eyes creased with concern and befuddlement.

As he put on the clean shirt and tucked it in his pants, Stillman told his wife everything he knew about the old lady's murder and the killer's attack on McMannigle.

"Does Doc Evans need any help with Leon?" Fay asked. She was sitting beside Stillman on the bed, who was now giving his boots a scrub with a damp cloth.

"Looks like he has everything under control. Besides, you have your hands full here." Stillman gave his head a jerk toward the living room.

"Yes . . . well . . . Candace is my student," Fay began tentatively. By the time she was done with the whole story, she was having to work at keeping her voice down, so angry had she become again at Earl.

"Let me get this right," Stillman said. "Crystal knocked Earl Hawley out cold in his own house?"

"And we tied and chained him in his own barn," Fay said, nodding.

Stillman thought it over, then shook his head and

gave a laugh. "Well, I guess the bastard had it
comin'. I'm not quite sure it's legal . . ."

"But I think it's high time he took Crystal's cure,
don't you?" Fay said. "After how he's mistreated
his family?"

"Taking Crystal's cure is no guarantee he's going
to stay off the booze, and it certainly doesn't mean
he's going to suddenly change hide color."

"No, but what other choice did we have? What
would you have done?"

Stillman thought about it. He shook his head
again, ran a hand across his bristly jaw, and chuckled. He looked at his wife, her pretty face flushed
from anger. "I . . . I guess I would have done just
what you did," he had to admit, and kissed her
cheek.

He got up and started for the door. "Well, I have
to get back out there. With Leon over at Doc's, I'm
going to have to spend the night at the jailhouse and
keep an eye on the town."

"You don't want supper? I have a roast in the
oven."

"No, I'll grab something over at Sam's. I feel I
should be as visible as possible. I can keep an eye
on the jail from there, too." He turned at the door
with a sigh.

"You look exhausted," Fay said, getting up and
walking to him. She put her arms around his mus-
cular torso and pressed her head to his chest.

"Not too bad. I'll get my second wind after supper and a pot of coffee."

"You be careful. I don't like your being alone out there."

"I'll be fine, Fay."

"Who could it *be?*"

Stillman sighed again. "I don't know. But I'm going to find out."

He bent down and kissed her lips, taking her head in his hands.

"You don't mind Mrs. Hawley and Candace spending a few days?" she asked.

"Not at all," Stillman reassured her. "Hell, I doubt I'll even be home that much. They'll be good company for you. Remember to keep the doors locked."

Fay smiled. "Thanks, Ben."

Stillman frowned. "For what?"

"For . . . just being Ben Stillman," she said. "The man I love."

He chuckled. "Right back at you, Mrs. Stillman."

He kissed her and left the room. On his way out of the house, he bid good evening to Mrs. Hawley and Candace, reminding Fay to keep the doors locked. Walking up the street to First, he paused and looked along the town's main thoroughfare, a dusty, wheel-rutted, hoof-pocked trail between two rows of false-fronted buildings. Night had come down and the wind had gentled, but it was cold.

West up the street, light spilled from the windows of the Drovers Saloon, the office of the Clantick

Courant, Auld's Livery, and Sam Wa's Café. Two horses stood before the saloon. Several more and a buggy sat before the restaurant. Shadows from the restaurant's window flitted on the boardwalk, which had been decorated with Halloween pumpkins and here and there a straw witch or goblin.

Here were the good, everyday people of Clantick who wanted only to live their simple, hardworking lives safely and comfortably, to feed their families off an honest day's wage, to attend church every Sunday, and to raise their children in harmony with all the other law-abiding citizens of Clantick. But they would go to sleep tonight uneasy, not sure that their homes were protected from a madman with a knife.

Who knew his reasons, or when he would stop? Hell, maybe he was done and had gone home, never to be heard from again. Or maybe he'd strike again tonight. Maybe, right now, in a quiet house on the other side of town, he was lurking outside a window . . . waiting. . . .

Unconsciously, Stillman's hand strayed to his revolver, and he fingered the butt. This was one of the few times in his turbulent life he'd ever felt comfortable enough with a town to call it home. As well as he thought he could ever fit in anywhere, he fit in here at Clantick. He liked the people and was proud to protect them, to give them the security they all deserved, even here in the untamed West.

But he wasn't doing that now. The killer was beating him and would beat him again and again, until he understood the man's motivation. Only then could he bring the good citizens of Clantick back under his umbrella of safety and security and reassure them once again that the world—at least this small part of it—was not a maelstrom. That it was an ordered, predictable place where they could fall asleep at night, reasonably sure they and their loved ones would awaken again in the morning.

Stillman gave a tired, frustrated groan and walked up the street in the direction he'd been gazing, past Carney's blacksmith shop, which was dark now, its doors closed. He went into Sam Wa's and saw that the place was three-quarters full. All voices stopped, all faces turned toward him.

"Evenin', Sheriff," someone said.

"Evenin' Ralph," Stillman replied, heading for one of the few free tables, feeling the crowd's expectant, questioning eyes on him.

It was the publisher of the Clantick *Courant*, a young Easterner named Evan Danielson, who gave voice to what was on all of their minds. "Any leads yet, Sheriff?" the slender man in the wire-rimmed glasses asked, turning around on his counter stool, a cup of coffee in his hands.

"Nope," Stillman said. Evelyn Vincent was filling his coffee cup, and he looked at her, tried a smile. "Do you ever take a break?"

"I usually go back to the boarding house for a nap

in the afternoon, but there's been so much commotion lately, bringin' people in from the country to hear the news, that Sam's needed me all day."

"Well, I hope to have the town back to normal in a day or two," Stillman told her.

The newsman cleared his throat and opened a notebook. "I was told just an hour ago, Sheriff, that you promised the city council you would resign if you did not find the killer by Saturday. Is that correct?"

"News sure travels fast."

The exchange set off a commotion as the other customers exclaimed to each other, most of them nodding their heads. "We can't have this man roaming the streets for two more weeks!" the gunsmith, Julius Hallum, said to his wife. They sat at a nearby table.

"I say you deputize ten men and scour the streets night and day for the sumbitch!" another man interjected.

"They'd just shoot each other," Stillman groused.

A man sitting beside the newsman raised his hand like a schoolboy. "I volunteer my services, Sheriff. I rode posse with Ralph Merchant back when the bank was held up two years ago."

"I'll think on it," Stillman said, wishing for a quiet place to eat his meal but knowing these people were only venting their fear and frustration. He had to allow them that and not take offense. He'd rather see this than an armed mob taking to the streets.

A tall man in a frock coat stood and regarded Stillman severely. "I think the killer is that new wop butcher we have in town, Sheriff!"

"Oh, why's that?" Stillman asked tolerantly, as Evelyn set before him a pound of marbled sirloin and fried potatoes on a heavy white platter. Stillman hadn't eaten for hours, and his mouth watered at the juice pooling in the pocks and swales of the aged, grass-fed beef.

"He's up and about at all hours of the day or night, and he knows how to use a knife."

"I'll talk to him, Fred," Stillman said, aiming his fork at the man. "But you leave him alone, you understand?"

The man's face flushed as he slouched back down to his seat.

Jeff Carney, the blacksmith, was sitting near the window, his wheelchair pulled up to a table, his big forearms raised over his plate. "A couple Injuns passed through here the other day, Ben," he said. "They needed a wheel fixed. They could be campin' down by the river and comin' into town at night, doin' the killin'."

"What would be their motive, Jeff?" Stillman asked.

"I don't know, but one of 'em was wearin' an awfully big knife."

Chewing a forkful of beef, Stillman pondered it, then shook his head. "No, I think it's someone who lives here, Jeff. I don't think it's an outsider."

"Whatever you say, Ben."

"Oh, by the way, Jeff, while I think of it, can you get to Sweets again tomorrow? That shoe you put on him came loose."

"First thing in the mornin', Ben. Where is he?"

"Stable behind the jail."

"I'll send a boy for him."

"Thanks, Jeff."

The newsman slid off his stool and walked over to Stillman, a notebook and a pencil held before him. "How's your deputy doing, Sheriff?"

"I'm going to head over to Doc Evans's in a minute and find out," Stillman said.

"Is there a chance he might have seen the killer's face?"

Stillman tore a hunk of bread off the small loaf in the basket beside his plate and swabbed grease from the platter. "Well, that's what I'm hoping."

The newsman sat down and leaned across the table toward Stillman, a conspiratorial light entering his gaze, a wry grin shaping his mouth. "You must have some idea who the killer is, Sheriff."

Stillman swallowed a mouthful of food and sat back in his chair, lacing his hands across his belly and scrutinizing all the faces around him. He brought his gaze back to the newsman. "For all I know at the moment, he could be you, Mr. Danielson." It was true, and the feeling the knowledge gave the lawman was one of poignant dread and frustration.

Looking chagrined, the newsman scowled. He was about to push himself to his feet when Stillman put a hand on his wrist, holding him there.

"Will you print a notice for me, Evan?"

The newsman lifted his eyebrows. "What kind of notice, Sheriff?"

"I'd like anyone who knows of anything that the four victims had in common to pay me a visit. A common thread ties the four together, and if I can find out what that thread is, I'll be all the closer to finding the killer."

The newsman nodded. "I'll get right on it, Sheriff. The new *Courant* comes out tomorrow. I'll see that it's on the front page."

"Obliged, Evan."

The newsman scribbled a note, stood, and went out. Stillman was scrubbing the last of the grease from his plate when hooves thumped outside and boots clattered on the boardwalk. The door opened, and the windburned face of a drover appeared.

"It's the killer, Sheriff!" the man yelled as his excited eyes found Stillman. "We got him!"

13

"WHAT ARE YOU talking about, Ed?" Stillman asked the drover.

The room had exploded when the drover first appeared with his surprising news but had fallen just as suddenly quiet, no one wanting to miss a thing.

"Me and the boys seen him ridin' to town on our way back to the ranch," the drover, Ed Jule, said. He worked at the Halliman ranch east of town, along the Milk River, and had spent a few nights in the calaboose for fighting over at the Drovers, the cowboys' favorite saloon. The smallish, sandy-haired man in a filthy cream hat with a corrugated brim was so excited he could barely get his words out.

"Go on," Stillman said.

The man stammered, shuttling his gaze self-consciously between Stillman and the watchful room. "Well, we seen him, that's all, and we was goin' to go ahead and string him up, but then Denny said I should go get you first. To make it all official."

"Yeah, I'll say you should get me first, for crying out loud," Stillman groused, wiping his mouth with his napkin, shoving his plate away, standing, and donning his hat. He headed for the door and the cowboy, saying, "What in the hell makes you think you have the killer?"

"Well . . . 'cause we seen him pret' near every night for the past week, ridin' into town on an old cayuse . . . wearin' a big knife on his belt. A Bowie knife!"

By this time, Stillman was out on the boardwalk, the cowboy trailing him. Behind the cowboy, all the customers in the restaurant were trying to squeeze out the door at the same time. Stillman turned to them, raising his hands.

"All right, all right!" he yelled. "Everyone just stay put and let me do my job."

"We wanna see ya string him up, Sheriff!" someone yelled.

"Yeah!" someone else responded.

The crowd roared, and Stillman was struck cold by the possibility that the mobs he'd seen before in other places would show up here. He drew his gun and squeezed off a round starward. "Anyone following me and Ed here is going to get ventilated, plain and simple."

With the bark of the .44, the crowd had silenced.

Now they stood there in the door, faces pressed to the plate-glass window, looking peeved but cowed. Holstering his revolver, Stillman said, "Show me where you've got this fella, Ed."

As the cowboy mounted his horse, Stillman untied a set of reins from the hitchrack and swung onto a jittery skewbald. "Whoever owns this horse can pick him up back here in a few hours. Much obliged." He swung the horse and cracked the steel to him. "Let's go, Ed."

"This way, Sheriff," the drover yelled importantly, reining eastward at a trot that quickly rocked into an all-out gallop.

Although the skewbald was wary of its alien rider, Stillman managed to keep the horse's head aimed forward as he encouraged its reluctant gallop. He followed Ed Jule on the wagon road east of town. About a mile out, Jule reined his horse off the road onto a horse trail that cut through scrub country southeast.

They rode up a butte and down the other side— Jule riding with the swiftness of a man who knew the trail in the dark, Stillman with the lurching uncertainty of a man for whom not only the trail but his horse was unfamiliar. It was rough, broken country, difficult enough in daylight, and Stillman did not want to roll the horse in a wash.

Finally, the trail descended a dry ravine, and Stillman and Jule were nearly upon the two other riders before Stillman discerned their hatted, rough-hewn features in the darkness. Jule reined his black to a halt, and Stillman did likewise, casting his gaze over the cowboys, both of whom he recognized as Drovers regulars, then at the man standing nearby with his hands tied behind his back.

He was a smallish man in an oversized canvas coat and a floppy-brimmed sombrero. His horse was tied to the trunk of a cottonwood only a few feet away.

"Okay . . . what the hell's going on?" Stillman demanded, keeping a tight rein on the prancy skewbald. He would have liked nothing more than for these three cowhands to have stumbled upon the killer, but he knew it was too much to hope for. There was no way the killer Stillman was after would let himself be caught by three drunk drovers heading back to the ranch after lighting it up in town.

"We been seein' this guy pret' near every night on our way back to the ranch, Sheriff," said Denny Blue, Mike Halliman's ramrod. He was a big, rangy man with a badly pitted face and hollow cheeks, as though he'd lost his back teeth. He talked as though around a mouthful of chaw. "We seen him carryin' a knife, an' since we heard those people in town had their throats cut by a big knife . . . well . . ." He let his voice trail off.

"You saw him carrying a knife, huh?" Stillman carped. "That's your sole reason for thinking he's the killer?"

The third rider, Deuce Jekyll, cleared his throat. "No, it ain't, Sheriff. I mean it ain't the only reason. When we yelled to him and told him we wanted him to stop so we could talk to him, he lit out like a bat out of hell!"

"Let me see the knife."

Denny Blue produced the knife from his belt and handed it to Stillman, who hefted it in his hands.

"See there—it still has blood on it," Blue said. "You want we should go ahead and grow some fruit on this here cottonwood?"

Stillman turned to the man on the ground, head down, the brim of his sombrero hiding his face. "What do you have to say for yourself, mister?"

The hat came back as the chin rose. "I—I didn't kill nobody!" The voice was that of a young man just on the windward side of puberty. In the darkness Stillman had to squint to make out his hairless face, wide across the cheekbones, narrow through the jaw.

"What's your name?"

"Chancy Ray. My pa and ma and brothers and me farm over in Mill's Hollow."

"What are you doing out here?"

"I . . . I'm goin' to town," the boy said reluctantly, voice rocky with young manhood and thick with emotion. He lowered his head again and stifled a sob.

"What for?"

The boy was silent, contemplative.

"Out with it, boy!" Stillman demanded.

Again, the chin came up. "I—I'm going to Clantick to see a girl." The chin dropped again to the boy's chest.

Gazing at the boy, Stillman thought about it. One of the drovers said, "She-it." Stillman ignored him. To Chancy he said, "What are you doing with this knife?"

"It's my huntin' knife," the boy said, looking at the ground. "An old man, a trapper my pa knew, gave it to me before he died. I wear it on me for . . . for luck."

"She-it, Sheriff."

"Shut up, Denny," Stillman growled. To the boy, he said, "A girl, huh?"

The boy nodded.

Stillman turned to the drovers. "You boys go on back to the ranch, and stay there. Don't let me see you in town for a week."

Deuce Jekyll was flabbergasted. "But, Sheriff, we—"

"You heard me, Deuce. If I catch you in town within a week, I'm going to haul you into the calaboose and turn the key on you. And if you ever pull a knot-headed stunt like this again, I'm going to fill you so goddamn full of holes you won't hold a teaspoon of water!"

"But—"

"Git, goddamn it! Git!"

Indignant and cursing, the men kicked their horses southeastward along the trail, Denny Blue

pausing to look back at Stillman and point at the
boy. "Don't let him wool you, Sheriff. That there's
the killer!"

Stillman drew his revolver and fired into the air,
smoke puffing against the black velvet of the starlit
sky. In a clatter of hooves, the three drovers were
gone.

Stillman turned to the boy. "Turn around here,
Chancy." The boy did as he was told, and Stillman
reached down with the bowie and sliced through the
ropes tying the boy's wrists.

"I'm going to hang onto the knife until I'm sure
you're as innocent as I think you are, Chancy," he
said. "Mount up and let's head to town. We're going
to find that girl you're supposed to be visiting and
put this thing to rest once and for all."

"I can't do that, Sheriff," Chancy said.

"What's that?"

"We . . . we ain't s'posed to be seein' each other.
I mean . . . her aunt don't know, and wouldn't like
it if she did."

"Why's that?"

"Well . . . if you knew her aunt, you'd know."

Stillman was too weary to inquire further. He just
wanted to get the kid on the trail to town, see the
girl he was supposed to be meeting so he could, in
good conscience, turn the kid loose, and get back to
work. "You have two options here, kid," Stillman
said tiredly. "You can either take me to this girl or
spend some time in the hot box. It's up to you."

The kid considered this. "Will you tell her aunt?"

"I don't care about her aunt. I just want to know you're innocent of murder."

The boy swallowed heavily, nodded, turned, and mounted his horse.

They entered Clantick twenty minutes later, and Stillman followed the boy and his knock-kneed cayuse to an old log barn behind a shack on the south end of town. The boy tethered his horse to the poles holding up an awning on the north side of the barn and headed for the doors. Stillman followed, coming up behind the boy as he pulled one of the two doors open, and stepped inside.

"Chancy, where have you *been?*" sounded a girl's voice, in a thick Norwegian accent.

Chancy hemmed and hawed, stepping aside for Stillman, who entered the smoky, dark quarters lit only by a single lamp in the girl's hand. Stillman's face warmed with surprise to see that the girl facing him, her clear blue eyes wide with shock, was none other than one of the Widow Bjornson's two nieces.

"Borghild?" he said, unable to conceal his surprise. Someone had mentioned in the café the other day how it seemed that Borghild was catching onto English so much faster than her sister Hilda. Stillman almost chuckled aloud now as he learned the reason why.

"Sheriff . . . I . . . I . . ." the girl stammered.

"Ran into your beau along the trail," Stillman said, hooking a thumb at the boy. "A couple drovers held him up, thought he was the man doing the kill-ing. I didn't think he was, but I had to make sure."

The girl had turned away in embarrassment, shielding the lamp with her body and casting Still-man and the boy in darkness. "It's okay," Stillman reassured her. "I won't tell your aunt. It'll be our secret. How would that be?"

As the girl turned back to face him, so did the lamp, though she held it lower than she had before. "Chancy, you got me in trouble!" she rasped, trying to keep her voice down. The barn belonged to Old Man Thompson, a widower and former dry farmer whose house sat about thirty yards south of the barn. He only used the barn for a stable and wagon shed these days.

"He's not going to tell, Borgy. Are you, Sheriff?"

"My lips are sealed," Stillman said. "How in the hell did you two meet, anyway?"

The boy shrugged. "Borgy's aunty sewed some clothes for my ma, and she and the girls brought them out one day." He flushed and shrugged again.

Stillman nodded, pondering this, smiling as he wondered how the Widow Bjornson would react to the news of Borgy's love affair. "Well, just don't set fire to the barn." With that, he turned to leave. "Oh, by the way," he said, turning back to the two young people who had come together, the lamp be-tween them. "You two be careful." He knew he didn't need to mention why. Everyone knew about the killer.

The boy turned a grin on Stillman and held up his knife. "That's why I got this," he said.

Stillman wagged his head, touched his hat to the girl, and left. Outside, he heard Borgy give Chancy a cuff. Chancy grunted painfully, but by the time Stillman was on his horse and reining toward First Street, he heard the muffled sound of a girl's giggle from within the barn's dark interior, where the lantern light no longer shone through the cracks in the boards.

He smiled fleetingly, remembering the long night he had ahead of him.

14

LEON MCMANNIGLE AWOKE early the next morning, just after dawn, and groaned.

He felt as though his head had been split with a dull ax. He brought his hand up to the thick band of tightly wrapped gauze. His mind was so foggy that he had to look around the unfamiliar room for several seconds, thinking hard, to remember what had happened and realize he was in Doc Evans's house.

"That sum*bitch!*" he cursed aloud, referring to the man who had hit him.

His fervent hiss loosed an arrow of pain through both temples. When the pain abated and he thought about it, however, he realized he was lucky to be alive. The man had come up and blindsided him, knocking Leon out so quickly that he hadn't even gotten a look at the attacker.

Why had the man not killed him? Whatever he'd

hit the deputy with had put him out like a blown candle.

Leon heard something outside his door. It sounded like a chair squeaking as someone rose. The floor barked with leather-soled footfalls. The door opened a crack. After a second it opened all the way, and Doc Evans entered, a shadowy figure in a vest and rolled shirtsleeves, in the misty dawn shadows.

"I bet I could drink two quarts of the Drover's cheapest snake water and not feel half as bad as you feel," Evans said wryly.

The deputy brought his hands to his temples, which had hammers in them, pounding away at his skull. "Oh, lord . . . you got no idea."

"I'll bring you some tea for the pain. It'll be a moment." Evans turned to go.

"Wait . . . how'd I get here?"

"Auld found you and threw you into a wagon."

Leon probed the bandages again, inspecting the damage. "What'd he hit me with, anyway?"

"A singletree. You're lucky it didn't crack your skull—not badly, anyway. Auld walked in as the man was about to cut your throat."

"Did Auld see him?"

"Not his face. It was too dark in the barn. Said he took a shot at him but missed. The man was rather fast on his feet. I take it you didn't see him, either?"

"Not his face."

"Let me get that tea."

The doctor went out and returned five minutes later with a stone mug that burned Leon's hand until he got his fingers through the handle. The steam wafting up, ghostly in the pale light angling through the curtained window, smelled like pepper and weeds. "What the hell is this?"

The doctor sat with a sigh in the chair beside the bed. A cigarette dangling from his lips, he scratched a match on the dresser. Touching the match to the cigarette, he said, "Herbs. My own concoction. It'll kill the pain."

Leon sipped the pungent brew and made a face. "A shot of whiskey is what I need."

"Not after the brain scrambling you've just incurred," Evans said, blowing smoke at the match flame. "This is better."

"You probably drank all the whiskey your ownself."

Evans offered a rare smile. "You're damn lucky to be alive. Mrs. Miller didn't fare so well."

Leon was taking another sip of the tea, which he'd found soothing in spite of its weedy aroma. "What's that?"

Evans took a long pull off his cigarette and told McMannigle about the death of Mrs. Miller, about how the killer had been spooked by the hired girl and jumped out the second-story window of Frederick Miller's house.

"That's probably when you ran into him," he said.

McMannigle shook his head and gave a sigh. "What a tinhorn I am."

Evans shrugged. "Bad luck. He jumped you."

Leon paused, staring straight ahead, the tea steaming in his hands. At length he turned to Evans. "Who is this guy, Doc? Who could he be?"

"It seems we have a Claudius on our hands."

"Who?"

"Never mind," the doctor said, running his hands down his blond-whiskered face, which Leon always thought much too civil-looking for a frontier doctor. "I've spent the night reading Shakespeare at the kitchen table."

"Reading who?"

Evans sighed and shook his head. "Drink your tea."

"I've had enough tea," Leon said, tossing back his covers and, in spite of the increased pressure in his skull, swinging his legs to the floor.

"Hey, hey, hey," Evans said.

"Hey, yourself, Doc. I got a job to do."

"Not today."

"Hand me my clothes," Leon said, indicating the jeans and shirt hanging over the back of Evans's chair.

"Not a chance."

Leon stood in his long johns, feeling a little unsteady, but reaching for his clothes just the same. The doctor stood his ground. "You get your ass back in bed, or I'll pistol whip you."

"Give me my clothes, Doc," Leon ordered.

The doctor stared stubbornly into the deputy's equally stubborn eyes. Realizing there was nothing he could do to keep the man in bed if he did not want to be there, he scowled, turned, and left the room.

Leon retrieved his clothes and gun belt from the chair and dressed, taking his time so his head would not explode, which it felt very close to doing. He knew he should stay in bed and heal, but he just couldn't do it. He'd had the son of a bitch trapped in Auld's barn and had let him get away. Now the man was free to kill again, and when he did, it would be Leon's fault. That's why Leon had to catch him.

Now. Today. He didn't have time for healing.

But how did you catch a madman? Stillman thought the man was operating logically, killing those he specifically wanted dead. But what if Ben was wrong? What if he was just a lunatic killing willy-nilly . . . just for fun?

How in hell would you catch him then?

If only McMannigle had seen his face. But all he'd seen was a tall, rangy figure in a dark hat and dark canvas coat. How many of those did you see on any given day on First Street in Clantick?

When Leon was dressed, he walked outside and saw the doctor waiting at the end of the walk in his old, battered buggy, his overweight chestnut hammerhead in the traces. The doctor wore a bear coat and wool hat against the freezing dawn air, and his cheeks were pink below his wire-framed glasses. A fresh stogie drooped from his lips.

"Get in here, goddamn it," he groused. "I don't have all day."

"I can walk, Doc," Leon said, gently settling his black Stetson on the exposed nerve of his head and wincing with the effort.

"And I'd let you walk if I thought you'd make it to the jailhouse. But the odds are you'd get halfway there, pass out, get run over by a ranch wagon, and I'd be up all night tending you again. Now get your ass in here."

When he was settled on the buggy seat next to the droll Evans, McMannigle turned to the doctor and said, "Doc, you're one charmin' fella. Anybody ever tell you that?"

"Not in this life," Evans groused and slapped the reins against his horse's back. "Onward, Faustus. Onward."

Ben Stillman turned the corner past Edgar Tempe's barbershop and headed west on First.

It had been a long night, and every hour was ta-tooed on his haggard, unshaven face. He wore a sheepskin coat and deerskin gloves, and his Henry hung barrel-down from his right hand. The collar of his coat was pulled up against the below-freezing cold, and his ten-gallon Stetson was pulled low on his head.

He'd walked every street of the town so many times the dogs had finally stopped barking at him. Before midnight he'd pounded on a dozen doors and informed the occupants of the situation. He'd warned them to keep their doors locked, their eyes peeled, and to spread the warning to their neighbors. He also cautioned them against shooting unless they were certain their lives were in immediate danger. Stillman didn't want to have to cart anyone but the killer up to the undertaker's tonight.

Fortunately, he hadn't had to. And as far as he knew, the killer hadn't struck. He regarded that as a plus in his column, but then again, he hadn't found the bastard, either.

He came to the jail and sat on the bench shoved up against the window, laying the rifle across his thighs, removing his gloves, and fishing in his coat pocket for his makings sack. Slowly, he built a cigarette, deciding his next course of action was to cable all the sheriffs in the surrounding counties and inquire about similar situations in their jurisdictions.

He knew it was a long shot, for this killer seemed to have an agenda specific only to Clantick, but what the hell? You could always get lucky. He had no other leads and nothing else to do but wait for someone to read his plea for help in the *Courant* and come forward with information, giving him the killer's motive and thus the killer himself.

That was probably a long shot, too. As Frederick Miller had so haughtily put it, what could a mulatto whore and an old Prussian immigrant woman have in common? But it was the only shot Stillman had, aside from waiting for the bastard to strike again and hoping he left some incriminating clue.

Stillman pulled on his cigarette and watched Sam Wa step out of his café across the street, broom in hand. The Chinaman saw Stillman, waved, grinned, and turned to sweeping the boardwalk before the café. Wa was always the first businessman on First Street in the mornings, and Stillman found himself scrutinizing the stout Chinaman suspiciously.

For a Chinaman, he was big; broad through the shoulders, thick in the arms. And as a cook, he certainly knew how to wield a knife. But what would be his motive? Why would Sam Wa, one of the most successful businessmen in Clantick—not to mention the most ostensibly humble—want to kill Cadena Martin, Hansel Hagen, and Mrs. Miller?

He heard the clip-clop of hooves and turned his head to look eastward down First. A cowpoke appeared there, coming up one of the north-south side streets, no doubt leaving one of the brothels, heading back to the ranch. He'd just left a warm bed and a girl, it appeared. His shoulders were hunched, his head pulled down against the cold.

As he rode away, Stillman scrutinized him as well, and decided against waylaying the man. He could tell it was Carl Witherspoon, a cowboy up from Texas, and Stillman had beaten him at cards

enough to know he wasn't nearly cunning enough
to be the killer.

But maybe this killer wasn't cunning at all.
Maybe he was just a madman preying on whatever
victims proved most convenient. . . .

Stillman dropped the quirley stub between his feet
and ground it out with his boot, shaking his head.
He couldn't say exactly why, but he just didn't think
so. As he stood, hefted the rifle, and went through
the jailhouse door, he hoped he wasn't just wishful-
thinking. A cunning killer with an agenda was easier
to find than a madman killing haphazardly for
thrills—once you figured out the agenda, that was.
With a madman you either had to hope for witnesses
or the good fortune of catching the man in the act.

Or woman . . . Could it be a woman? he mused,
tossing his hat on the peg behind the door. No. Few
women would be strong enough to sink a knife that
deep and pin poor Hansel Hagen to his barn door.

As he added paper and kindling to the glowing
coals in the potbellied stove, he heard hoofbeats ap-
proach and stop, and he lifted his head to see Doc
Evans's carriage out the window. Frowning, Stillman went to the door. McMannigle was climbing
gingerly down from the buggy.

"What the hell's going on?" Stillman groused,
sliding his eyes between the two men.

"He's chomping at the bit to catch your killer,"
Evans said.

Leon straightened, looking pale behind his mahogany skin, his face wan. He gave a mock salute. "Leon McMannigle reporting for duty, Sheriff."

"Get back to bed."

Leon dropped his arm. "I'm fine. Besides, you're gonna need help today."

"Not from you. Your brains are scrambled."

Leon touched his head. "Gotta head like black Norwegian marble. I'm ready to go. Really."

Stillman looked at the doctor. Evans shrugged, shook his head, and slapped his reins against the old horse's back. As he clattered down the street, Stillman took McMannigle by the arm. "Get in here," he said and led the obviously weak deputy through the door and planted him in the swivel chair behind his desk.

"You idiot," Stillman groused. "You should be in bed. You're no help to me in this condition. You need at least another day's rest, maybe two."

Leon gave his head an easy wag. Stillman could tell his eyes weighed a ton. "I'm fine, Ben. I have to catch this guy. I had him in there . . . in the barn . . . and let him get away."

"That could've happened to anybody."

"It never happened to me before, and I fought Apaches for five years in Arizona." His cloudy eyes found Stillman. "You don't think I'm losin' my edge, do you, Ben?"

"No, I think your brains are scrambled," Stillman said, then turned back to the stove and saw that his paper and kindling had burned out. He needed to start again.

"How'd it go last night?" Leon asked, as Stillman tossed a crumpled newspaper in the stove.

"All was quiet." Stillman suddenly stopped what he was doing and turned to Leon. "Say, you didn't get a look at him, did you?"

McMannigle shook his wobbly head. "Sorry. He came up behind me, and . . ."

"Yeah, I know—lights out. Don't worry about it. Auld was there, too, and he didn't see his face, either. It was too dark in the barn."

Leon winced. "I feel like a goddamn fool!" He winced again as pain shot through his head.

"You are a fool—for not staying in bed," Stillman chided him.

While he worked on the fire and set coffee to boil, he told Leon of the notice in the *Courant* and about his plans to cable the sheriffs in the surrounding counties.

"I'm going to have Fay cancel school until we've caught this guy—if she hasn't already, that is," he said. "Best keep all the young'uns to home. I have a feelin' it's going to look like a ghost town around here, now that the word is out. I doubt many businesses on First Street will open, and that's all right." He poked at the fire and shuttled his gaze to Leon, who was fast asleep, head thrown back in the chair, hat falling back against the wall.

Stillman sighed and shook his head. He was about

to throw Leon over his shoulder and ease him onto
a cot in one of the cells when he heard footsteps
outside. Turning, he saw the door open and two girls
from one of the brothels walk in on a draft of cold
air, their faces flushed, uncombed hair falling around
their shoulders. It appeared they were fresh from bed
after a hard night's work and hadn't bothered to
straighten themselves. They wore wool shawls over
gray night wrappers.

"Leon McMannigle, what in the hell do you think
you're doing?" one of them piped, a sandy-blonde
with a mole on the right side of her mouth.

Leon jerked awake and reached up to catch his
hat. "Huh . . . what . . . ?"

"Doc Evans stopped by and said you'd gotten out
of bed!" the other girl carped, arms folded across
her ample bosom. "You—in your condition!"

"Girls, please," Leon begged, the sudden stir of
emotions lighting another fire in his head. "I have
work to do." He slid a sheepish glance at Stillman.
"This is my official base of operations. The sheriff
and I were just discussing strategies to—"

"Oh, don't give us any of your official hogwash,
Leon," the sandy-blonde said, grabbing one of
Leon's arms. "You're coming to bed with us. We'll
feed you and cuddle you and keep you warm until
you're all better and ready to go back out and fight
the bad men—won't we, Rachel?"

"Be our pleasure, Leon," Rachel said lustily, tak-

ing McMannigle's other arm and gently heaving him
out of his chair.

Stillman stepped back, smirking, watching the
doctor's scheme worked to perfection by the two
lovelies from the brothel Leon called home.

Standing, one girl on each side of him supporting
him, Leon turned to Stillman. "Ben, I . . . I guess
you're right," he said weakly. "I think I do need a
few more hours in bed."

"I think you made the right decision, Deputy,"
Stillman said with a mock-official nod.

"I'll be in after a nap," Leon said as the girls led
him out the door. "You . . . you take care of yourself."

"You, too, Leon," Stillman called after him, shut-
ting the door behind him.

He'd turned back to his desk, grinning, when the
door opened again. He turned to it and saw the girl
Rachel standing there, clutching her shawl about her
slender shoulders. "How 'bout it, Sheriff? Wanna
come, too?"

Stillman laughed and shook his head. "Thanks,
anyway."

"You'd be surprised how many married men we
entertain," Rachel said, lifting her eyebrows entic-
ingly and dropping the shawl, offering a liberal view
of her cleavage.

"No man married to a woman like mine," Stillman returned with a smile.

The girl frowned and turned. As she headed out

the door, she said, "Spoilsport," and closed the door behind her.

Outside, the girls ushered Leon east down the street and north at the first corner. Crossing the side street, they entered one of the three brothels sitting side by side and led their patient up the narrow, squeaking staircase. McMannigle had finally succumbed to his condition; the thought of spending a few hours in the sheets with these lovelies helped a great deal to convince him that was exactly what he needed.

Leon was a regular in the brothel, which had no name but was simply identified by its shingle over the street as Rooms by the Hour. He lived here, in fact, and his color, unusual in these parts, had won him a lordlike status. He did not pay rent, nor for professional services. The madam and her girls wouldn't hear of it. His mere presence prevented the ugly trouble that occurred in most houses of ill repute. That, his gentlemanly demeanor, and his regular gifts of something frilly for the girls were payment enough.

"Here we go, Leon," Rachel said, removing the deputy's hat and depositing him on the bed. "Let's just help you out of those duds and get you all tucked in here," she cooed like a mother hen. "There we go, that's it," she said as she and Penelope each removed a boot.

"Ah, girls, girls . . . my head hurts," Leon whined, characteristically unashamed of his boyish behavior in the presence of such genuine love and affection.

"Oh, I know it hurts, but it won't for long. . . ."

At length, McMannigle was naked and lying on his back, feeling the pain abate significantly as the two girls undressed before him. When each was naked and had stoked the stove in the corner, they crawled into bed with him, making the bed squeak, their soft breathing like the flapping of angels' wings, their naked breasts and legs and hands brushing his skin until he fairly groaned with sensuous pleasure, all his nerves alive—all, that is, but the injured ones in his head.

Rachel knew exactly how to dull his pain further, leaving not even a trace, and when she finished, she brought her head back up from the sheets, gave his cheek a motherly kiss, and curled up against his chest while Penelope snuggled up against his back.

In moments, all three were fast asleep.

15

EARLY THAT SAME morning, Fay walked into the living room of her and Ben's little house on French Street and saw Candace standing at the window, one hand parting the curtains, and staring out at the dimly lit street under a soft, opalescent sky. The girl's head was turned slightly, and Fay saw that her expression was as sad as always.

"Candace," Fay said, "how would you like to take a walk with me?"

The girl turned to her expectantly. "To school? Isn't it too early?"

Fay set the breakfast plate she'd been drying on the table and shook her head. Reluctantly, she said, "I'm sorry, Candace, but there won't be any school today." It was almost funny, she thought, how no school could be bad news. But to this child who had little else, that's exactly what it was.

The girl seemed to understand at once. Without expression, she said, "It's the bad man, isn't it?"

"Yes," Fay said, frowning. "How did you know?"

"I heard you and Momma talking last night after I went to bed. He's not after us, too, is he?"

Fay knelt before the girl, gazing into the child's injured eyes. "What do you mean, 'too'? Who else do you think is after you?"

The girl looked at her hands. Her voice was as thin as a dry leaf rustle. "Poppa."

"Oh, child . . . your father isn't after you."

"Yes, he is . . . and he'll be lookin' for me and Momma . . . 'cause we went away . . ."

Fay bit her lip, perplexed. How do you discuss such matters with a child, so that she'd understand and not be afraid? On the other hand, why shouldn't she be afraid? Earl Hawley could very well break out of his barn and come looking for them.

Fay now knew what it was that had haunted the girl's dreams last night, causing her to scream and her mother to comfort her in her bed. Thinking of the killer preying on Clantick, Fay had reached for the shotgun by the bed. She'd made sure both doors were locked, but then she'd realized, hearing Mrs. Hawley's soothing tones, that Candace had been having a nightmare about her father.

Staring at the child's big, brown, downcast eyes, Fay mused that a child should not have nightmares about her father. About killers, yes, but not fathers. Fay's stomach clenched with anger all over again, and she wished Ben were here to help her support this injured child and mother. She suddenly felt as lonely as Candace must feel, trapped in this big, deranged, adult world.

"Your father is not going to hurt you, Candace," Fay said resolutely. "I promise you that."

Candace's eyes went to Fay's, but there was no solace in them. She said nothing, and her silence was like an indictment. Fay could not protect her forever from fathers and killers. And Fay suddenly felt naive for believing this child, having seen what she'd seen of this adult world, would believe her.

"Now, about that walk . . ."

"If there's no school, where we going?" Candace asked.

"I have to go downtown and get someone to inform the rest of my pupils there won't be school until the killer has been caught—which I expect my husband to do in the next day or two."

Fay heard Mrs. Hawley clear her throat behind her. "I thought we was s'posed to stay inside," she said, frightened. "Your husband said we shouldn't go out."

Fay stood and turned to Mrs. Hawley, who stood wringing her hands in the hall. Fay didn't like the idea of leaving the house any better than Mrs. Hawley did, but she saw no other choice. "I have to go out," Fay said, "and I think it would be safer if we all went together than if you and Candace stayed home alone. We'll only be gone for a minute."

Mrs. Hawley's hand strayed to her bruised, gaunt face. "I think . . . I think we should go home," she said thinly, her eyes darting around the room as if searching for an escape route.

"No," Fay said, louder than she'd intended. She walked to the woman and took her hands in her own. "You're just frightened. But you know that home wouldn't be any safer than being here with me."

"Oh, I . . . I . . ." the woman said, stricken eyes filling with tears.

"No, Noreen," Fay cajoled her. "You have to be strong. You have to be strong for Candace."

"Please, Momma," Candace cried, running to her mother and throwing her arms around her waist. "I'm afraid of Poppa. I wanna stay here with Mrs. Stillman . . . until he's all better and won't hurt us anymore."

Noreen Hawley gazed down at her daughter. She lifted her hand to the girl's face and pressed the hair away from Candace's eyes. Her own eyes had settled down, the terror gone from them, replaced by resignation. She nodded.

"Okay, child," she said.

Then, lifting her eyes to Fay's, she said it again. "Okay."

"Okay," Fay echoed with relief. "Let's get ready for our walk now, shall we? I bet we can even pick up some material at the mercantile for a new dress. How would you like that, Candace? We'll spend the day baking cookies and sewing you a new dress."

Candace's tired eyes found Fay's and offered a smile.

"All right, then," Fay said, turning toward her room. "Bundle up good, it's cold out there."

In the bedroom she found her heavy wool cape, gloves, and earmuffs. She also found her gun and dropped it in a pocket of the cape. She just hoped she wouldn't have to use it.

But she would, by God. If that madman showed himself, he'd be a hell of a lot worse off than Earl Hawley.

When Jody Harmon had kissed his wife good-bye and headed out to help his neighbor dig a well pit, Crystal finished washing the breakfast dishes and sponged off the table. Then she filled a picnic basket with leftovers from last night's supper and this morning's breakfast, shrugged into her red-plaid mackinaw, donned her hat, grabbed her Colt rifle, and headed out to the barn, where she saddled the black mare she called Angry Ann, due to the mare's intolerance of stallions. Crystal might have been a simple country girl in some respects, but she was not without irony, and she thought it appropriate that she ride Angry Ann on this particular morning's errand.

She'd ridden a mile toward the Hawley farm when she came to a dim wagon path descending a shallow, wooded draw. Crystal halted Angry Ann, considered the intersecting trail for a minute, then abruptly reined the horse upon it, following the dim ribbon down the draw, through a thin stand of aspens, and up a saddle. Descending the saddle, she rode into the yard of an abandoned ranch headquarters, the house, barn, and corrals overgrown with weeds and falling into ruin.

She halted Angry Ann between the house and corrals and sat there silently regarding the cabin, the stoop of which sat askew, its steps overgrown with witchgrass and Russian thistle. The windows were broken, and most of the shakes were gone from the roof, leaving only the rusted coffee cans Crystal's father had pounded flat and used to fill the holes.

As Crystal sat there regarding the forlorn place, the cabin suddenly grew back its shakes, the stoop straightened, the windows filled with unbroken glass, and the weeds disappeared. Smoke lifted from the chimney, and the door abruptly opened.

Crystal's father, Warren Johnson, suddenly appeared. His face and wide, broken nose was red with rage. Clutching a fifteen-year-old Crystal by an arm, he jerked her out of the house and heaved her down the porch steps into the yard. The young Crystal lay in the yard, sobbing, while the big, staggering man poked an arm at her, shouting, "I ever hear you been seein' that half-breed Harmon kid again, I'll pull your goddamn pants down and tan your ass but good!"

The girl screamed and twisted around to her father. "You can't make me," she cried. "I love Jody!"

"Why, you goddamn little slut!" Johnson roared. He started off the porch.

Crystal's mother came through the door and grabbed his coat, pleading, "No, Warren . . . *please don't!*"

Johnson wheeled, bringing a big red fist up and smashing it into the side of his wife's head. She screamed, slammed against the doorframe, and sank to the porch.

Johnson turned back to Crystal, stumbled down the steps, regained his balance, and grabbed her hair. Lifting her head, he swung his right hand back. He'd started bringing it back toward Crystal's face when, sitting atop the mare, Crystal squeezed her eyes closed and turned away.

The image was gone but not the sound of Johnson's hand connecting with her face and the ensuing scream.

The sounds began to fade only when Crystal had ridden Angry Ann around behind the cabin and pointed her across the pasture, toward a knoll upon which a grave sat, marked by a homemade cross. Crystal reined the horse to a stop before the cross and gazed down at the grave, humped with rocks to keep the coyotes and wolves from digging up the bones.

Her father was buried here, and she did not come here often. Warren Johnson had drunk himself to death after killing Jody's father, Bill Harmon. Crystal's mother and siblings were scattered to the four winds by Warren Johnson's drunken fury.

Crystal sat staring at the grave for a long time,

trying to calm herself. Then she said, frowning and shaking her head, sucking back tears, "Why?"

Only the chill autumn wind rustling the dry grass answered. Crystal knew it was the only answer she was ever going to get.

Finally, she reined the horse back the way she had come and was soon on the trail leading to the Hawley farm. Twenty minutes later, she rode into the farmyard, Angry Ann shying at the dog, which ran out from the porch to bark and growl.

"Oh, quit," Crystal grouched at the dog, dismounting. She tied the reins to the corral, and when the dog saw that Crystal wasn't afraid, it slunk back to the porch and lay on the top step looking Crystal's way and pricking its ears.

Crystal unstrapped the lunch basket from behind her saddle, dipped a hand under the lid, and produced a handful of beef bones wrapped in paper. She unwrapped the bones and tossed them toward the house. "Here you go," she said, and the dog came running.

Crystal hesitated a moment before opening the barn doors. Suppose Earl Hawley had gotten loose? She considered grabbing her rifle and decided against it. If he was loose, she'd have seen him by now.

Grunting as she heaved open the doors, the barn smells wafting over her, the milch cow giving a startled low, she squinted her eyes to see into the shadows and stepped cautiously forward.

She'd taken two steps when "Who's there?" barked from the stall where she and Fay had chained and tied Earl Hawley. Crystal nearly sighed with relief. He hadn't gotten loose. He was still safely chained to his stall.

"It's Crystal," she said, moving forward.

"Get over here, you sassy bitch . . . *and turn me loose!*"

"I'm not turning you loose, but I will feed you," Crystal said.

She stopped at the stall, looking over the four-foot-high partition. Hawley sat with his back against the barn wall, both hands tied with stout hemp to chains secured to metal rings in the wall. The man's face was sweat-streaked, his thin, brown hair damp and matted against his head and flecked with hay. His wrists were bleeding from his attempts to break the ropes.

"Turn me loose, you goddamn whore!"

Crystal froze. Her father had called her that, a long time ago, when he'd first heard that her childhood friendship with Jody had grown into courtship. A film of red anger lowered over Crystal's eyes like a drawn shade. Her jaws tightened.

She fairly trembled as she said, "What did you call me, Mr. Hawley?"

"I called you a goddamn Injun-lovin' whore!" The force of the rebuke had pushed Hawley away from the wall. Its aftermath sent him back against it, staring into Crystal's eyes. He seemed pleased with the reaction his words had evoked. His upper lip rolled slightly in a grin.

With barely bridled anger, Crystal dropped the lunchbox, turned, and left the barn. She returned a half minute later with the Colt carbine she mostly used on coyotes and snakes and to discourage any lecherous cowboys she ran into on her trips to town. She levered a shell in the chamber and stepped up to the stall, bringing the rifle butt to her shoulder. She aimed the barrel at Earl Hawley's head.

"Hey, hey," Hawley said, bland eyes growing wary, looking at her askance. "What . . . what ya doin' there? Be careful with that goddamn thing!"

Crystal pulled the trigger. In the enclosed quarters, the rifle's bark was like a twice-amplified hammer strike. Smoke puffed around the receiver.

Earl cried out, recoiling and squeezing his eyes shut. The bullet drilled a ragged hole about six inches left of his head.

The rifle barked again, Earl cried again, recoiling, and cracked an eyelid to see the hole the bullet had torn into the wall six inches right of his head. "Y-y-you're goddamn crazy!"

Crystal lowered the carbine. "My father once called me what you just called me, Mr. Hawley. That's when I left home and never again took time for the son of a bitch. He was a drunk like you. He died a drunk—alone, his whole family hating him, hating him still. His life was nothing because of the bottle. Just like yours."

Crystal gave a ragged sigh and shook her head. "You have a chance to change now. I suggest you take it. Unless you want to end up like Warren Johnson."

She looked at Hawley. He looked back at her, eyes glazed with fear, anger, and newfound respect. A sweat bead carved a deep runnel down his face, plowing through his beard. He didn't say anything.

Crystal bent down and picked up the lunch basket. She tossed it over the partition into the stall, where it landed with a slap and a wicker squeak, the cover coming off, its contents rolling out.

"There's food . . . if you're hungry," she said. "There's a canteen of water in there, too."

"You're crazy," he snarled.

Crystal turned and headed for the white-faced milch cow regarding her warily. Behind her, Hawley yelled, "Where's my wife and kid?"

"Safe," Crystal said.

"You can't do this to me, you crazy bitch! When I get outta here, I'm gettin' the sheriff. You just see if I don't!"

He went on with his tirade while Crystal found a stool and a pail and milked the cow. When she was half finished, Hawley's invectives turned to pleas. Once he even sobbed.

"I . . . I promise I won't drink no more. You just have to let me out of here. Please. I—I can't take it out here. It gets cold at night and . . . and . . . I'm lonely," he sobbed.

"You're going to get a lot lonelier, Mr. Hawley." Crystal kicked the stool away and set the milk pail in Hawley's stall. "This'll help you keep your strength up. You're gonna need it. I have a feeling today and tomorrow are going to be right tough."

She turned and headed for the barn doors. "Either I or Jody'll be over again tonight to milk the cow and see how you're getting along."

"Why are you doing this?" Hawley asked, voice heavy with frustration.

Crystal stopped and pondered this. "Because I know what your wife and daughter are going through, and because I wish someone had done it for me and my family." She swallowed and walked away.

"You have no right to do this to me!" Hawley shrieked.

It was a penetrating cry, and it pricked the small hairs on the back of Crystal's neck.

She turned at the doors. "Maybe I don't, Mr. Hawley," she said, "but I'm gonna do it anyway. Maybe someday you'll thank us for it."

With that she was gone.

Nearly a half mile from the farm, she could still hear Earl Hawley ranting and raving from within the barn, and she wondered if he would change or end up like her father—first alone and unloved, and then dead.

She sniffed, and only then did she realize she was crying at the waste of it all, the horror, wondering what her family would be like now, if only her father hadn't been a drunk.

It was getting on toward late in the afternoon when McMannigle awoke again and found himself alone in bed. He looked out the window. Seeing that the sky was darkening, he figured Rachel and Penelope had gone downstairs to prepare for the evening.

He shoved himself up against the pillows and took stock of his condition. His head hurt, but the pain was nothing like it had been only a few hours before.

He shook his head and grinned. Those lovely ladies had given new meaning to the old saw "just what the doctor ordered."

Then suddenly his heart hammered in his chest and his temples were set to pounding again. He stiffened, raised slowly up in bed, his dark eyes widening in shock and surprise.

On the mirror of the dresser across the room were soaped the words Gess Hoose Next?

16

THAT EVENING, FIRST Sergeant Anlon Flaherty ran pomade through his hair with both hands and combed the thick cinnamon mane until the teeth tracks fairly glistened, tipping his head this way and that in the chipped mirror hanging above the washstand. Finished, he exchanged the large comb for one a tenth its size and went to work on the big red mustaches poking up on either side of his freckled slab of a face.

"What you got going tonight, Sarge?" Corporal Edwin "The Toad" Todd asked Flaherty as he went to the stove and poured a cup of coffee.

Todd had been reading an illustrated magazine on his cot when Flaherty had sauntered into the non-commissioned officers' quarters, freshly bathed from the bathhouse, and began dressing in the wool uniform he'd sent early the previous day to the laundresses on "suds row."

Only when he'd smelled the heavy, sweet pomade

did the feckless Todd remember it was Saturday,
and he realized the big Irish sergeant must have gotten an overnight pass and was heading into Clantick,
four miles northeast of Fort Assiniboine. Most Saturday nights, Flaherty finagled a pass and headed
for the little frontier berg and one of its gambling
dens or pleasure parlors, or both.

"Big game tonight, Toad. Big game."

"How come I wasn't invited?"

"On your salary? Ha!"

"You only make five dollars more a month than
I do, Sarge. Coulda asked me to tag along."

Flaherty put down the mustache comb, adjusted a
lock of hair over his left ear with his fingers, scrutinized his big, tobacco-stained teeth, and reached
for his gun and cartridge belt hanging on a wall peg.

"Sorry to say it, Toad," Flaherty said, sucking in
his profligate gut as he wrapped the belt around his
waist, "tonight's a little out of your league. I have
a game goin' above the Drovers with a doctor, the
chairman of the city council, and three First Street
businessmen. I squirreled into one of their games
last week on account of I know three of the five
from the pleasure parlors."

"Bigwigs, eh?" Todd said, reclining on his cot
with a sigh. "Screw 'em."

"That's just what I intend to do—just like last
week," Flaherty said, carefully donning his forage
hat in the mirror. He turned to the Toad reclining
on his cot looking very toadlike—*My God the kid*

had been hit with the ugly stick!—and showed his teeth again in a horsey grin. "Maybe I'll buy ye a beer and a Cuban cigar later."

"I don't need your charity, Sarge," the Toad groused, indignantly turning over his magazine.

Chuckling, Flaherty ducked through the doorway into the main part of the barracks, where a handful of enlisted men lounged on cots or stood around the the woodstoves shooting the shit. Fires popped in both stoves, and the warm air smelled like pine smoke, sweat, farts, and the proscribed beer the men often smuggled on Saturday nights. One of the men, sitting on a cot in his long johns, his back to Flaherty, brought a crock jug down from his mouth and casually slipped it between his legs.

Flaherty ignored it. Poor rats had to have something out here in the middle of friggin' nowhere. The sergeant had been on the Hi-Line nearly seven years and had grown accustomed to the empty solitude of the place. Even the winters. But then, when you had a clucking hen of a German wife and two squealing brats back in Deadwood, you figured you could handle just about any solitude God or man could throw at you—outside of the federal hoosegow, that was.

"I'm off, men," Flaherty called, lifting an arm. "You all stay halfways sober, ye hear. I hear from the Toad in there any of ye got drunk and started playin' grabby-pants again, I'll have the whole company drawn and quartered!"

As the men groused their exclamations and someone threw a boot, Flaherty turned through the door and stepped into the chill early evening, just enough light left in the sky to make out the officers' quarters, with their silhouetted gables and white picket fences across the parade ground. If he'd stayed with the butcher's daughter from Deadwood and his two brats—and if he'd minded his p's and q's—Flaherty might have been living over there himself, a pair of lieutenant's bars on his shoulders.

But then he might as well be six feet under, because that would be the end of his fun. Two years of that at Fort Meade had shown him how a hundred-fifty-pound woman could turn a two-hundred-fifty-pound Irishman into a pile of steaming dog dung, and he'd have no more of that horse hockey!

Flaherty took a deep draught of the air spiced with wood smoke and decaying grass and leaves, and reached for the reins of the horse he'd had saddled and brought over from the stables.

He walked the chestnut across the parade ground, then left the compound between the stables and granary, kicking his mount into a lope over the gently undulating hills lifting north and east of the fort. He picked up the main road connecting the fort with Clantick about ten minutes later and followed its twisting course along a dry creek bed. He watched the stars growing brighter as the sky grew darker and noted the eerie whoop of a bat.

When he thought he was a safe distance from the

fort, he lifted his chin and threw both lungs into a hoarse, ludicrously bass rendition of "The Gambling Man," his horse pricking its ears nervously at the big, vociferous Irishman on its back, the man's face tipped up toward the winking stars.

Sergeant Anlon Flaherty liked nothing so much as the prospect of skinning an uppity bunch of small-town bigwigs, and skinning them so badly they'd have little choice but to invite him back again next week for more. Ha!

"Oh . . . I'm a rambling gambler . . . I've gambled all around. Wherever I meet with a deck of cards, I lay my money down. . . ."

The Irishman sawed back on his reins, bringing his horse to a sudden stop and tipping an ear to listen. He'd heard something . . . or thought he had.

He waited, hearing only the dry grass rustling along the trail.

"Help me . . . please," came a voice, riding the cool wind from Flaherty's right, from the dry creek bed.

"Who is it? Who's there?" the Irishman called.

"Help me . . . please. I've taken a fall. . . ."

The hair along Flaherty's spine bristled at the ghostly lament, barely discernible above the breeze and the leaves that blew across the trail. He was spooked and wary. Someone could actually be in trouble, but then bandits were known to haunt the trail between the fort and Clantick. A year ago, after payday, three soldiers were on their way to town with their pockets full. They were found several days later in a ravine—shot and robbed.

With his right hand, Flaherty unsnapped the cover over his army-issue Colt and hefted the gun in his hand. He took a breath. "Where are you?"

"Here . . . by the tree," came the voice, brittle with what sounded like genuine pain. "I've taken a fall. I think . . . I think my leg's broken. My horse . . . he spooked. . . ."

Flaherty looked around, pricking his ears and squinting his eyes. He considered leaving the man; he could very well be riding into a trap. But Flaherty had just enough conscience that leaving a possibly dying man along the trail on a cold autumn night could very well disrupt his poker concentration and cost him money. No, he had to see what this was about, damn it all, anyway. . . .

When he was reasonably certain no others lay in hiding around him, he said with a sigh, "All right, laddy. Hold on."

He reined his horse off the trail, the chestnut hesitating as it descended the crumbling clay bank and started through the tall grass of the creek bed. Flaherty made for the big, leafless box elder tree, standing in the center of the brushy creek bed, its crooked limbs ghostly against the starry sky, like a drawing from a child's Halloween storybook.

The Irishman coaxed the reluctant horse with gentle commands, prodding it with his heels. "You're by the tree, you say?"

"Yeah . . . you're headin' right. Much obliged." The injured man grunted painfully. "Didn't think anyone was gonna come along. Thought I was gonna have to crawl back to town."

The man's voice grew louder as Flaherty neared him. Finally, a hatted form took shape at the base of the dark tree. The Irishman reined his horse to a stop and looked around.

The injured man said, "Damn horse . . . he spooked at a hawk or somethin' . . . flying out of this tree here. He gave a buck and . . . I wasn't ready for it. Landed wrong and heard somethin' snap. Sure 'nough . . . think my damn leg's broke."

Again satisfied the man was alone out here, Flaherty gave another sigh and holstered his revolver. "All right," he said and dismounted with the grunts and blows of a portly rider. "Let me get a look at ye there."

He tied the horse to a low-slung branch on the other side of the tree and turned to the man sitting with his back against the trunk. He looked at the man's face but saw nothing but a dark shape against the darkness of the tree. The man grunted and gave little moans, barely heard above the breeze-brushed grass and the creaking limbs of the box elder.

"Which one is it?" Flaherty said, jerking his pants up his legs and dropping to one knee.

"This one here . . . it really hurts. You think it's broke?"

The Irish sergeant squeezed the man's leg in two
different places. "That hurt?"

"No . . . not there."

"Here?"

"Nope."

"Well, where then?"

The man ran his right hand down the injured leg,
stopping at the shin. "Right in there. Hurts somethin'
awful."

Flaherty probed the shin with both hands. The
man sighed with pain. "Well, it doesn't feel to me
like it's broke. You prob'ly just twisted it good, or
cracked it, maybe." He turned his head to look
around. "Where's your horse?"

"He done run off, Anlon Flaherty," the man said,
in a voice that had turned surprisingly, suddenly
calm.

The sergeant jerked his head back to the man.
"You know me?"

"Of course, I know you. How could I not know
who you are?"

The hair along the Irishman's spine lifted once
again. He froze there, trying to make out the injured
man's face in the dark. "Well . . . you have me at a
disadvantage, then."

"The name Dalton Bliss mean anything to you?"

"Bliss?" Flaherty said, cocking his head and
squinting his eyes. "Bliss . . . ? Yeah, it does ring a
bell. . . ." It did, but he could not recollect where

exactly he'd heard the name before. All he knew, unconsciously, was that his hands in his gloves were turning soft and sweaty and his heart was beating erratically.

"How 'bout Danny and Jim? Those names mean anything to you?"

"Danny . . . and Jim . . . ?"

"It was a sunny fall day, just like the ones we been havin' lately, and those two boys were swingin' in the breeze," the man said, ominously. His voice was now clear and even, horrifically sane.

Flaherty wanted to reach for his revolver, but his hands wouldn't move. He knelt there, hands on his knees, staring at the dark shape against the darker shape of the tree, his brain shuffling half-remembered images: two young men hanging from ropes, from a tree much like this one here . . . their bodies swinging in the autumn breeze . . . leaves blowing . . . a crowd gathered and watching. . . .

"You're . . ." Flaherty tried, but his voice was a bursting bubble in his throat.

"That's right," the man said.

The sergeant stared at the man, frozen, unable to wrap his mind around the moment. Then suddenly he brought his right hand up to his gun. It wasn't there. He jerked his head down to find it—the holster had slipped farther back on the belt.

As his eyes found it, so did his hand. But by the time he got the revolver out, it was too late.

His head came up just as the knife cleared his throat.

"That's for those two boys . . . swingin' in the breeze," were the last words Anlon Flaherty heard on earth.

17

IN A DREAM, Stillman was chasing the killer down an endless maze of streets. Houses lined the streets, and the townspeople stared out the windows at him with admonishing looks on their faces, shaking their heads.

He ran up one street and down another, the killer remaining about fifty yards ahead of him—a vague figure in a dark canvas coat and floppy-brimmed hat. At one point Stillman closed the gap to about ten yards, so that the sheriff could see hair flapping on the man's collar, the stitching in his coat.

Then the killer turned the corner around a porch where the little girl, Candace Hawley, sat on a glider holding a doll. Stillman rounded the corner and found that the killer had increased the gap between them again to at least fifty yards, but running at an infuriatingly steady pace.

Try as he might, Stillman could not catch up to the man—corner after corner, house after house,

street after street, while the townspeople watched
from their windows and shook their heads in dismay.

Then he saw a woman—it was Evelyn from Sam
Wa's Café—laughing at him and pointing. He
stopped in his tracks and looked down.

He was buck naked!

Waking from the dream with a start, he bounced
in his office chair and lifted his head.

"Oh, did I wake you?"

It was Fay. She stood on the other side of his
desk, looking ravishing in a black wool poncho upon
which rich coils of black hair tumbled. She wasn't
wearing a hat, and her cheeks were rosy from the
cold. What a contrast Stillman's gorgeous wife was
to the dream he'd just been having.

"No," he said, clearing his throat and removing
his boots from the desktop, where he'd placed them
when he'd decided to steal a few minutes' shut-eye.
McMannigle was patrolling the town, and Stillman
was tending the office, keeping a fire going and the
coffee hot. "No . . . I was . . . having a nightmare, I
reckon." He chuckled, remembering it.

"What kind of nightmare?" Fay's gloved hands
clasped the handles of a small wicker picnic basket,
which sat on Stillman's desk smelling of warm food.
Her eyes, etched with concern, were on her husband.

Stillman chuckled again, bent over, and ran his
hands through his thick hair, which badly needed a
trim. "I dreamt I was chasing the killer through

town—naked as a jaybird." He shook his head.

Fay arched an eyebrow. "Well, that's certainly one way of doing your job, Mr. Stillman. You know what that means, don't you?"

"I reckon I'm wired a little tight these days."

"And you feel that, because you're having trouble finding the killer—for completely understandable reasons, I might add—you're standing naked before the town."

Stillman pursed his lips, nodding thoughtfully. "Well, I reckon I am. And I reckon they find me a little lacking in places."

"Only in the dream, dear heart." Fay smiled her smoky smile, and its effect went deep into Stillman's loins.

"Come here," he said.

Moving around the desk, she removed her gloves and knelt between his knees. He bent forward and took her in his arms, lifting her off her knees and holding her close, running his hands down her back. She buried her head in his chest and sighed. "Oh, Ben . . . we haven't been together in days."

"We see each other now and then."

"You know what I mean."

"Yeah," he sighed, squeezing her, burying his face in her hair. "I know."

"What are we going to do? I can't be away from you any longer. It's making me crazy."

He smelled deeply of her hair. It smelled like lilacs. It made him yearn for spring, picnics in the mountains, making love under the aspens with their new green leaves. "There's nothing we can do . . . until I find the killer."

"I hate that son of a bitch."

Reluctantly, Stillman removed his face from Fay's hair, placed his hands on her shoulders, and gently eased her away. "I'm sorry, Fay," he said. "I wish I could tell you I'm close to catching him."

"Your notice in the paper hasn't helped?"

Stillman shook his head. "No one's come forward to help us connect the victims." Stillman sat back in his chair, still clutching Fay's hands in his. "Until they do . . ."

"You're sure there is one . . . a connection?"

"I'd bet my life on it."

They remained there, gazing into each other's troubled eyes, Stillman sitting back in his chair, Fay kneeling between his knees, her hands swallowed by his. He brought himself slowly forward and kissed her rich, full lips, loving the taste of her, wanting more, but . . .

He pulled away, a suddenly troubled frown wrinkling his brows. "Hey," he said, "what are you doing here, anyway?"

She stood and moved toward the basket on the desk. "I brought you breakfast: two sourdough biscuits with scrambled eggs and bacon. They're probably cold by now, but—"

"You shouldn't be leaving the house alone," Stillman admonished her.

"I didn't leave alone. Mrs. Hawley and Candace are with me. I left them over at the café." She gave a devilish smile and patted her hip. "Besides, I'm packing iron."

Stillman shook his head, half-smiling, as Fay brought the food out of the basket and unwrapped it. "You didn't have to do this. I could have gotten breakfast over at Sam's."

"You've eaten plenty at Sam's. I know Sam is a very fine cook, but you need a meal cooked by your wife on occasion. It's about the only intimacy we've had in longer than I care to think about."

"Sure smells good," Stillman cooed, tucking a napkin into his shirt and staring down at the two sourdough biscuits she placed before him. The smell of fresh bread, bacon, and eggs wafted up on steam tendrils. "Still hot, too."

"I tried to wrap them tight, right out of the oven."

While he ate, Stillman asked Fay how her guests were doing.

"I feel so awful," Fay said. "I thought bringing them to town would be best, since Candace could go to school with me. But now that school's been called off because of the killer, we're just sitting around baking and working on a dress."

"Well, hopefully ol' Earl will mend his ways." Chewing, Stillman chuckled and shook his head. "I don't see how he has much of a choice, with you and Crystal adjusting his attitude for him."

Fay was about to reply, but just then someone

knocked on the door. It was a kid who ran errands
for the businessmen around town. He'd led Stillman's horse, Sweets, back from Jeff Carney's blacksmith shop, a new shoe on its right rear hoof.

"Much obliged, Charlie," Stillman said, when
he'd inspected the hoof. He tossed the kid a dime.
"Spend a penny of that on your favorite candy."

"Thanks, Sheriff," the twelve-year-old lad replied
with a grin. He was about to turn away when he
remembered something. "Oh, here's the bill."

"Obliged," Stillman said, intending to place the
scrawled note with others he'd give the city council
at their next gathering.

"See ya, Mr. Stillman," the kid said, jogging off.

Stillman had intended to tell the kid he should be
indoors somewhere, safe from the killer running
loose, but he knew it wouldn't have done any good.
Charlie's father was dead, and his mother was sick
with consumption. The family lived in a little shack
down by the river, not far from the mulatto's place,
and young Charlie was the family of five's sole
breadwinner. If he didn't work, the family didn't eat.

Stillman turned to Fay, standing in the open jailhouse door holding a cup of coffee. He'd just started
toward her when he heard thundering hooves and
clattering wagon wheels approaching from the west
on First Street. He looked that way and saw a buckboard wagon barreling toward him. A few seconds
later, he could make out the two figures on the seat:
Jody and Crystal Harmon, dressed for the cold in a

sheepskin coat and a red plaid mackinaw respec-
tively, their hats secured to their chins by leather
thongs. Their faces were cold-rosy, their expressions
grave.

Both Stillman and Fay stepped into the street as
Jody pulled the two horses to a halt before the jailhouse. "Now, what's got *your* fur standing on end?"
the sheriff asked, his face gaunt with weariness.

Jody set the brake. His voice was urgent. "We
came on the west road to town—you know, the one
that goes by the fort? I needed some lumber, and
Crystal wanted to visit Fay and check on Mrs. Hawley and her daughter. Anyway, we're a mile or so
past the fort when we see that there soldier layin'
dead smack in the middle of the trail."

Turning around on the wagon seat, he indicated
with a nod the dead, blue-clad soldier lying in the
empty box of the lumber dray. Stillman had already
seen the man and was looking him over.

"Goddamn," Stillman groused. "Sergeant Flaherty."

"You know him?" Jody asked.

"He comes to town every Saturday for poker.
Quite a character. I played a few hands with him
myself." Stillman shook his head ominously. "His
throat's been cut, same as the others."

"The killer?" Crystal said. She'd craned around
in the wagon seat next to Jody, holding her collar
over her ears, her blond hair blowing about her face.

"Looks like," Stillman said. "What the hell . . . ?"

"I left a bandanna tied to a stake where we found him, if you wanna have a look," Jody said.

Stillman's arms were crossed over the side of the wagon box. He was studying the dead sergeant, the man's head bare, his auburn hair and ostentatious mustaches sliding around in the wind, his throat cut, just like the others, to the bone. Stillman made a fist and dropped it to the wagon's sideboard, gritting his teeth.

"Who's next?" he said. "Who in the hell is next on this madman's list of victims?"

"Maybe me." It was Fay.

Stillman jerked his head to her. She stood beside him, regarding the dead man with grave eyes, her face pale.

"What are you talking about?" Stillman said almost angrily. How could she joke about such a thing?

"I don't know why I never thought of it before. It just now occurred to me." Fay turned her gaze slowly to Stillman, an odd smile on her lips. "I know what the connection is."

Stillman studied her for a moment. She was dead serious. She really did think she knew.

When Stillman finally found his voice, it was almost a whisper. "What?"

"About five years ago, when I was living on the Hi-Line with Donovan Hobbs, I took the stage to Sydney to visit one of my aunts who'd recently moved there. On the way back, the stage was chased just outside of Malta by two young men with shot-guns." She stopped, her eyes darting around unsee-ing, thoughtful, trying to recall it all.

"And . . . ?" Stillman said, impatient.

Fay slid a lock of hair from her eyes with a gloved hand. "There was a Wells Fargo agent riding shot-gun. When the driver speeded up the stage to try and outrun the two would-be robbers, the agent fell overboard. He was trampled by one of the gunmen's horses and killed. . . . That scared the boys. They left the stage and ran, but the Clantick sheriff at the time, and a posse, tracked them down. The driver, myself, and the other four passengers on the stage testified against them at the trial. They hadn't been wearing masks—that's how young and stupid they were—so they weren't hard to identify."

Jody cuffed his hat back. "I remember that," he said. "The circuit court judge at the time was called Hang 'Em High Hank, and he hung those two kids right here on First Street—though it wasn't called First Street back then. Hell, it was the only street in town at the time."

"Oh, it was terrible!" Fay cried with a shudder. "If I would've known he'd hang them, I never would have testified against them. It was a crazy stunt they pulled, but they didn't mean to kill that man. They should have gotten a prison sentence, certainly, but not hung. They were so young; why, they couldn't have been more than sixteen or seventeen years old!"

Stillman was listening carefully, taking it all in. His heart beat rhythmically against his sternum. "And who were the other passengers?" he asked hesitatingly, not really wanting to hear any more but knowing he must.

Fay held up a gloved hand and splayed her fingers. "I don't remember all their names, but one was an old woman, who would be about Mrs. Miller's age now."

Fay bent her small finger down with her left hand.

"There was also a young man, a farmer who had just moved here. I can't remember his name, but I bet it was Hansel Hagen."

She peeled her fourth finger down.

"The third was a mulatto woman, traveling back from somewhere in Dakota, I believe, though I don't remember why, if I ever knew. She rarely talked— I think that's why I didn't remember her."

The middle finger went down.

"Sergeant Flaherty was the fourth person. I remember him quite well. How could you forget Sergeant Flaherty?"

Fay peeled down her ring finger, leaving her thumb, which she pointed at her breast, saying, "And the fifth person was me."

"Jesus God!" Stillman groused, unable to believe what he'd been hearing. His own wife could be the next target? "Are you sure about all this?"

Fay nodded fatefully. "Quite sure, I'm afraid." She looked at her husband. "I'm so sorry I didn't think of it before. It was just so long ago, and I never really knew the other passengers. . . ."

"I understand," Stillman said, deeply troubled. "I wonder why no one else in town thought of it."

"Too long ago, probably," Jody said. "The town and pret' near the whole county's been completely repopulated since then. I can only think of a handful of people here now—besides Fay, Crystal, and me— who were around back then."

Stillman nodded. He cast his thoughtful gaze downward, still not wanting to believe it was true. "We still can't be certain about the connection." To Fay, he said, "You're not sure Mrs. Miller and Hansel Hagen were the other two on that stage. It's a long shot, I know, but it may still not be the connection we're looking for."

"Yes, it is," Crystal piped up reluctantly, shaking her head with a grimace. Her expression was dull, her eyes flat. "I remember Hansel Hagen telling me one time he'd been a witness at the trial of the Bliss boys—that was their name. Bliss."

She let her voice trail off, her eyes meeting Fay's. "I'm so sorry," she said.

Jody looked at Stillman. "So, you think it's someone avenging the Bliss boys?"

"Sounds like it to me," Stillman said with a sigh. He knew that Fredericka Miller had to have been a witness, as well, and that Fay was indeed right about the connection being the hanging of the Bliss boys. He was suddenly so sure that he didn't even feel the need to confirm it with Mrs. Miller's son, Frederick.

Fay looked at him and sighed. She lifted her lovely black brows ironically. "The fishing gets better when you find the right bait," she said.

Stillman was incredulous. "What are you talking about?"

"If you're going to catch the killer, you're going to have to bait him, my sweet." Fay shrugged. "I guess we both know what—or who—he's going to try biting on next."

Stillman opened his mouth to give a fervent reply, but Jody cut him off. "What about the driver of the stage? He must have testified, too, didn't he?"

Crystal shook her head. "Ol' Billy Emory died from a cancer two summers ago. He drank with my pa."

"That just leaves me," Fay said to Stillman, a wistful smile pulling at her mouth.

Ignoring her, Stillman looked from Jody to Crystal. "Will you two do me a favor? Take Sergeant Flaherty up to Doc Evans, then come back to Sam Wa's and pick up Mrs. Hawley and her daughter, and take them back to your place. Will you do that?"

"Sure," Jody said.

"What about Fay?" Crystal asked with deep concern etched around her eyes.

"My darling wife is going to the safest place in town," Stillman said with resolve.

"Oh? Where's that?" Fay asked, crossing her arms over her breasts defiantly.

"The hoosegow," Stillman said to her. Gesturing to the jailhouse door, he said, "You're under arrest. Git!"

18

EARLY THE NEXT morning, Stillman walked down First Street toward the jailhouse. Looking around at the false-fronted buildings lining both sides of the street, he saw that all was quiet. Too quiet. It was only seven A.M., and only Sam Wa was normally open this early, but it had been practically this quiet all day yesterday and probably would be all day again today.

There had been an ominous note to the quiet, like a held breath between screams.

People were staying home out of fear of the killer's knife. Several merchants hadn't even opened their stores. What was the point, if they weren't going to draw more than a handful of customers? And who knew they wouldn't be a target in their own businesses, end up with their throats slit, blood draining out of their severed jugulars?

Most of the people on First Street the last few days had been cowpokes, heading for the saloons.

They weren't afraid of any hombre with a knife. Just let the bastard try to pull a stunt on them like the one he'd pulled on Sergeant Flaherty!

Stillman looked behind him, eastward down First Street, at the dark shapes of the two-story, wood-frame buildings, the gray blue morning light silhouetting them against the kindling dawn sky. Dry, wind-blown leaves scuttled against the south-facing boardwalks and gathered in small, rust-colored drifts. Paper blew up in the alleys. The Halloween decorations in some of the windows didn't look so much festive as taunting.

Stillman sighed. The killer had struck only a week ago, but in that time Stillman had aged considerably. The covert son of a bitch had sapped him worse than any gun-brandishing cowboys could have done, shooting up the town on a Saturday night. The killer had sapped him worse even than Donovan Hobbs, who'd tried to rustle the Hi-Line blind a few years back.

Even during his eighteen years as deputy U.S. marshal of Montana Territory, Stillman had never encountered anything like this: a man killing one person after another, seemingly indiscriminately. Knowing the method behind the man's madness was only a partial balm, because he also knew now that his own beloved Fay was a target. And nothing in the world could have made him feel more frustrated and angry and vulnerable.

If anything happened to Fay . . . if that madman

got to Fay ... Stillman didn't know what he would
do short of murder. Certainly, he would lose his
mind.

Because of his deep aggravation this morning, the
chill, wind-blown First Street he saw was a darkly
malevolent place, cloaking a killer after his wife.
After a cursory gaze westward, where a wagonload
of pumpkins sat before the loading dock of Hall's
Mercantile, Stillman turned to the jailhouse, opened
the door, and went in.

He got a fire going and went over the cables he'd
received from other sheriffs, the last few days. The
boys who'd held up the stage had been from Malta,
so Stillman had cabled the sheriff there, asking for
the names of any and all relatives. He'd gotten a list
of five, but none of the names matched anyone he
knew here in town, which wasn't surprising. If
someone related to the boys was going to take up
residence here and blend in well enough to start killing Clantick citizens without anyone suspecting him,
he sure as hell wouldn't use his real name.

He did find out a few interesting things, though.
One was that the judge who had hung the boys, the
honorable Henry Amos McCallum, Jr., aka Hang
'Em High Hank, had been killed two years ago behind a barbershop in Jordan, in eastern Montana. His
throat had been cut.

Stillman smiled at the cable and shook his head.
He had to admit that ol' Hank had probably got what
he deserved. But those who'd testified against the

boys certainly had not. And whoever was doing the killing, no matter how grief-stricken and crazy he happened to be, was going to pay for his sins.

Stillman was thoughtfully stoking the woodstove a quarter hour later when the jailhouse door opened. Looking up, Stillman watched Frederick Miller and Rolph Garrity, chairman of the town council, walk in, removing their brushed beaver hats. Garrity shut the door behind them, turned to Stillman, and said, "Good morning, Sheriff."

Stillman dropped the poker in the wood box. "Mornin'," he replied without heat. He could tell by his visitors' grim expressions they were here to offer neither support nor encouragement. "What brings you out so early?"

"We want to know if you've gotten any closer to finding that madman," Miller said. His narrow face was pale, in sharp contrast to his black, upswept, carefully waxed mustache.

"I'm sorry, I haven't," Stillman lied, crossing his arms. Either of these men could be the killer.

Miller and Garrity shared a glance. Garrity turned to Stillman.

"We can't go on like this, Ben. I know it's only been a week, but another week of business—or its lack, I should say—is going to close most of First Street down. This killer is ruining the town. People are literally afraid to leave their houses, and if they can't leave their houses, they can't shop."

"I know exactly what you're saying, Rolph," Stillman said.

Garrity pulled at his thin gray beard and adjusted his spectacles on his big red nose. "The town council has called an all-town meeting this afternoon at one o'clock in the Boston. In light of the fact you haven't been able to find the killer—or come up with any viable leads—we intend to discuss our options."

Stillman sighed. "The first of which will probably be asking me for my badge."

Garrity shared another sheepish glance with Miller.

"I know it's not fair, Ben," Garrity said. "I personally doubt anyone else could do any better, but the businessmen on First Street are up in arms. I'm afraid they're going to vote we bring in someone else."

Stillman moved to his chair and sat down. He tossed his makings pouch across the desk. "I don't have any cigars. You men care for a cigarette?"

Garrity shook his head. Miller didn't move a muscle. He just stood there very stiffly in his crisp, tailored suit, his thin lips pursed with mute derision. Stillman knew he was the one, because of his murdered mother, fanning the flames of Stillman's removal from office. Stillman didn't blame the man for how he felt. If their roles were reversed under similar circumstances—if Fay had been killed, God forbid—Stillman would have felt the same way.

Outraged and lashing out at the closest available target.

Still, there was something unscrupulous about how the man used his wealth and power to manipulate the town council, and Stillman could not help disliking the man very much indeed.

Stillman rocked back in his chair. "Don't worry. I'll be at your meeting, and if I haven't caught the killer by then, you'll have my badge."

The men nodded and turned to go.

"Oh, Mr. Miller," Stillman said, as if the thought just occurred to him, turning the man back around. "By any chance, was your mother a witness at the Bliss boys' trial several years ago?"

Miller's eye slid warily to Garrity's, then to Stillman. "Why, yes. Yes, she was. Why do you ask?"

Stillman shook his head and shrugged. "Just curious, is all." He smiled.

The men looked at each other in conspiratorial silence, then haltingly left the jailhouse. Stillman heard them muttering on the other side of the door as they walked away.

They'd been gone ten minutes when Stillman heard a horse walk up to the hitchrack. Lifting his head to look out the window, he saw Fay, and got a bad case of the jitters.

Stillman got weak-kneed around his wife every time he watched her take her clothes off. The reason for his nervousness in her presence now, however, had nothing whatsoever to do with lust. It had to do with the possibility that he might lose her once again, as he'd done back in Milestown nearly a decade ago. The difference was that losing her now meant losing her forever.

Stillman could no more imagine his life without her than he could imagine the sun going out, casting the earth in darkness.

Before the glowing woodstove now, in the jail-house office, Stillman held Fay in his arms and kissed her deeply. At length, he held her away and gazed into her eyes. "Isn't there some way I can talk you out of this?"

Fay smiled. "You just want to keep me under lock and key for the rest of my life . . . do naughty things to me."

"Well, you'd be alive . . ."

Her expression turned serious. "I—we—can't live freely knowing he's out there. And the only way he's going to come out of hiding is if I lure him out. He must know me well enough to know that I go riding every Saturday morning about this time. He'll follow me. When he does"—she dropped her hands to her hips—"you'll nab him. It'll all be over and we can go back to our normal lives again."

Stillman shook his head. "I don't like it. Not a bit."

Her voice was urgent, persuasive. "Ben, he's brash. You said so yourself. That's why he went after Mrs. Miller in broad daylight and dragged poor

Sergeant Flaherty onto the trail, where his body would be easily found. He's killing for revenge, but he also enjoys it."

Fay shook her head. "That kind of daring will force him after me today. And, since we haven't told anyone about learning his motive, he won't suspect we're onto him. He won't realize you, Jody, and Leon will be out there, ready to grab him as soon as he makes his move."

"Well, it won't have to be much of a move," Stillman pointed out, squinting his eyes with anger. "All I have to do is see him on your trail and I'm nabbing the bastard. He'll have the murder weapon on him. That and the very fact he's following you will be enough to hang him." He punctuated the sentence with a sharp bob of his head.

"There you go," she said, caressing his cheek with her hand and gazing into his eyes. She smiled reassuringly.

"Did Leon and Jody head out?"

Fay shrugged. "Jody left the house right after you did. Leon walked me over here from the house and headed out. He should be in position soon."

Stillman sighed, slipped his revolver from its holster, and spun the cylinder, making sure all chambers showed brass. He knew Leon and Jody, who were taking up positions off the trail she always rode, would keep an eye on her. But when you were dealing with a madman, you couldn't be certain of anything.

"Well, I guess if we're going to do it, we'd better do it." He was frowning down at the gun in his hand.

"I don't like this any better than you do, Ben, but it's the only way."

"I reckon," he groused.

"I'll be going."

She turned to go. He grabbed her arm, pulled her to him once again, and kissed her. "You be goddamn careful," he ordered. "The first sign of trouble—"

"I know, I know," she sang. "I'll signal you with my gun."

"See ya, Mrs. Stillman."

She smiled broadly and pecked him on the cheek. "See ya, Mr. Stillman." With that, she opened the door and went out.

From the window he watched her mount her black mare, Dorothy, rein the horse away from the hitch-rack, and gallop eastward down First Street.

Stillman hurried over to the gun rack and plucked his Henry out from behind the chain. Poking cartridges down the tubular magazine under the barrel, he tried to calm himself. It would do no good to hurry after her. The killer might see him and savvy the trap. He had to give Fay at least a fifteen-minute head start.

She had a gun and a fast horse, he told himself. She was good with both. And Leon and Jody were out there with her. She'd be okay.

Still, the prospect of losing her made his heart skip beats and his pulse race. The minutes came and went like hours. Finally, the calendar clock over his desk struck nine.

He slung the Henry over his shoulder, tipped his hat brim low on his forehead, and headed out for his horse.

19

LEON MCMANNIGLE HAD ceased following Fay when he saw her walk into the jailhouse. Then he returned via the back streets to the Stillman house, retrieved his horse from Stillman's buggy shed, and traced a circuitous route southward from Clantick. He rode cross-country to avoid being seen on the trail that Fay would take later.

The deputy suspected the killer was already out here somewhere, lying in wait along Fay's trail, the way he'd lain in wait along Flaherty's trail from Fort Assiniboine. Or maybe McMannigle was only hoping he was, so they could catch the son of a bitch once and for all. He knew Stillman's job was on the line, which meant his own job was on the line, as well. None of it made a damn bit of sense, but those were the cards they'd been dealt by the ingrates on the town council.

Yes, the deputy thought, as his gray gelding climbed the steep cutbank of a dry creek bed. Something indeed told him the killer was out here . . . somewhere. Leon's years in the cavalry had given him a keen sense of danger, and that sense was working overtime this morning.

As he rode toward Squaw Butte, which sat just off the trail Fay would soon be riding, and where he'd take up his position with his spyglass, he remembered the note the killer had scrawled on Leon's mirror: "Gess Hoose Next?" A real cutup, the son of a bitch was. Real smart. He'd gotten a taste of the bloodlust, gotten a liking for the cat-and-mouse game, and was having a real good time. He might have started out a grief-stricken father or brother of the dead Bliss boys, but killing had come a little too easy for him. It had become more than a nasty chore.

It was downright an adventure. The only problem was, he'd become a little too adventurous. Today, when he'd make the mistake of going after Fay in broad daylight, it would all be over. Then he'd find out "hoose next."

Leon scowled, kicking his horse up the butte, setting his jaw at the pain the jolting ride produced in his tender noggin. He'd gotten his marbles pretty much back in their right pockets, and he was no longer seeing double, but his head still barked in protest to too much hocus-pocus. He hadn't told Stillman and Fay that, however, because he wanted nothing more than to be part of catching this guy.

Near the top of Squaw Butte, Leon hobbled his

horse in some boulders, where the gelding wouldn't be seen from below, and produced his spyglass from his saddlebags. He took the spyglass into a niche in the boulder-strewn top of the butte and hunkered down in a natural cubbyhole. From here, he could glass practically eighty percent of a five-mile stretch of the wagon road angling south from Clantick.

The sky was low and gray, with a hint of autumn rain in the air, and the breeze was out of the north. After taking a slow, careful gander of the trail and seeing nothing but the pale wagon road snaking across the undulating brown prairie, he lowered the spyglass and checked his pocket watch. Five minutes to nine. Fay should be in sight in a minute or two.

Leon lifted the spyglass again and aimed it northward, toward town. He thought he might be able to see Jody from here, but the young man was hidden from view. He would hole up in a shallow ravine until Fay had passed, then make a wide westward semicircle around the trail, keeping her no less than two or three hundred yards away from him. One of them needed to be fairly close at all times.

Leon watched and waited and nibbled one of the bacon and egg biscuits Fay had made him and Jody, for a midmorning lunch. He had to snort and shake his head, thinking how calm the woman had been. She'd been about to dangle herself before a crazy killer, but she'd baked those biscuits and scrambled those eggs and fried that bacon like it was just another Saturday, and she thought she might take a ride into the mountains later.

That was quite a woman Stillman had. Leon found himself wishing he'd find himself one similar, maybe settle down in a house and raise some kids. The problem was there weren't many unattached black women in these parts, and he didn't think it would be right to marry a white woman and put her through the prejudice he often experienced but had, in a way, learned to live with. Another problem he had was his attraction to whores and crazy people. They were interesting but not always the best marriage partners.

That got him to remembering Mary Beth, the name he'd given the crazy Indian girl who'd lived with him here on the Hi-Line, and who'd been killed by Donovan Hobbs's men two and a half years ago—in Ben Stillman's arms, as a matter of fact. Tears veiled his eyes. Admonishing himself for his sentimentality, he wiped them quickly away with his coatsleeve and brought the spyglass back up to his face.

As he looked northward along the trail, a horse and rider appeared, and Leon's heart quickened. He couldn't tell from this distance, but it had to be Fay. He held the spyglass on her, feeling his muscles tense as she rode his way, curving along the trail. She was closer to Jody now, but in about ten minutes or so she'd be passing Squaw Butte. Leon would watch her for another ten minutes, not letting her out of his sight, while Jody switched positions.

How would the killer attack? Leon wondered. *Would he spring on her from hiding, or would he just ride up real casual-like, smile, and start a conversation, try to catch her off guard?* It was probably someone they all knew, and he'd use that familiarity to try to disarm her. Stillman had warned her to be suspicious of everyone.

Leon stood tensed, ready for anything, as Fay came near enough that he could see her poncho and gloves, her hair flopping on her shoulders, the rabbit fur muffler on her head. His heart beat an insistent rhythm, but he really did not expect the killer to show himself until Fay was farther along the trail, a good distance from town, probably among the mountain foothills, where the killer could hide in the brush and trees.

Leon was right. It wasn't until long after he'd left Squaw Butte, riding behind Fay about fifty yards east of the trail, that he heard a rifle bark and a horse scream.

Stillman had been about to spur his horse up to Fay and call it off.

He knew this was her usual Saturday route, but they were getting too deep in the mountains, and the brush and trees were too thick for him, Jody, and Leon to keep an eye on her. He'd spied both men at different intervals, but they were having trouble keeping up with Fay as they negotiated the rugged, off-trail terrain. Even though she'd slowed consid-

erably for them, there was no way they could get to
her in a hurry if she ran into trouble.

Besides, it looked as though the bastard wasn't
going to show, after all. He'd no doubt spotted one
or two or all three of the men, and Stillman realized
it was virtually impossible to lure the guy out after
Fay *and* keep an eye on her at the same time. There
was no way to move out here without being seen.

It had been a nice try, but success just wasn't in
the cards.

He was making his way along a cattle trail, in a
ravine just below the trail Fay was on, when something moved about twenty yards ahead of him, beside a boulder half-buried in a knoll.

He'd just made out the head and shoulders of a
man aiming a rifle, when smoke puffed around the
barrel. The rifle cracked as the bullet tore into Stillman's left arm with an audible thud. The impact
twisted the lawman around on his saddle, and before
he knew it, the horse was sunfishing off to his right,
and he was sitting on air. The ground came up to
meet him with a violent womp, scrambling his
brains and making his ears whistle.

He rolled to his left, instinctively grabbing the
Colt off his hip. The rifle cracked again, tearing up
sod where Stillman had first hit the ground. Sitting
on his butt, knees bent, Stillman leveled the barrel
of the Colt at the figure once again bringing the rifle
to bear on him. Smoke and fire geysered from the
rifle, but not before it had stabbed from Stillman's

Colt. The sheriff's slug apparently hit home, for the rifleman's bullet hit a rock about five feet to Stillman's left.

The rifleman disappeared behind the knoll, and Stillman looked around for Sweets. Seeing no sign of the frightened bay, Stillman remained there on the ground and evaluated his right arm, from which blood issued, staining his sheepskin coat. The arm was on fire, but probing with his fingers, he detected both an entrance and exit hole. The bullet had gone clean through.

He climbed unsteadily to his feet, having injured his hip and knee in the fall, and stumbled over to the boulder. As he moved around it, gun out before him, he heard pounding hooves and rustling brush. Swinging a look to his right, he saw the horseman galloping up a natural levee.

Someone yelled. Guns popped. Then there was the sound of the hooves again, dwindling in the distance.

Stillman heard another horse approaching on his left. He turned and saw Fay barreling toward him on Dorothy. She swung the black mare off the trail and descended the ravine toward Stillman. She approached, her eyes wide with concern, her .32 caliber Smith & Wesson in her hand.

"What happened?" she yelled. "My God, you're shot!"

"It's not bad," Stillman said, coming around the boulder favoring his right hip, which felt as though someone had buried a knife in the joint. He was certain it was only bruised, however. If it were broken or dislocated, he wouldn't be walking on it.

Fay was on the ground, inspecting his arm. "My God, Ben—it looks bad."

He was looking around for Sweets. He had to follow the killer. Fay's life depended on Stillman's catching the man.

"Take your coat off," Fay ordered.

Stillman ignored her as he looked south, then east, staggering on his injured hip and knee. "I have to find my horse."

"Ben—"

"The arm's all right. I have to find Sweets!"

Limping, he ran a few yards back along his trail, then swung around and returned, shaking his head. He grabbed Dorothy's reins from Fay, gripped the saddle horn, and poked his boot through a stirrup.

When he was in the saddle, he held out his hand to Fay. "Come on!"

"Where we going?"

"To find Leon and Jody. I'm going to leave you with them; then I'm going to follow that bastard on Dorothy."

The earlier gunfire told Stillman that either Leon or Jody were on the other side of the levee. He spurred Dorothy that way, Fay's arms wrapped around his waist. When the mare had worked her way through the hawthorn and chokecherry bramble of the levee and descended the other side, Stillman saw both Jody and Leon. They stood beside Jody's horse, preparing to mount the line-back dun. Not far away, Leon's steel-dust gelding lay on its side, neck stretched in the dry grass, open eyes glassy with death.

"What the hell happened?" Stillman asked.

Flushed and agitated, both men had already swung their looks at the approaching riders.

"Bastard shot my horse!" Leon yelled. His eyes slid to Fay. "Are you all right?"

She tipped her head at Stillman riding in front of her. "He didn't get me; he got Ben. His arm needs tending."

"Later," Stillman said. "I'm leaving her here with you two. You can double up on Sweets . . . when you find him."

Knowing there was no arguing with her husband, Fay slid reluctantly but smoothly off Dorothy's back. Taking two steps back from the horse, she gave her worried eyes to Stillman.

"You be careful," she pleaded.

The words hadn't died on her lips before he was off in a fury of pounding hooves.

20

STILLMAN DIDN'T HAVE to follow the tracks far along the wagon road to realize the killer was heading back to town. He wanted to catch the man before he could slip back into the crowd, but it was no use. Stillman had lost too much time back where he'd been ambushed. The killer was a good ten minutes ahead of him, and ten minutes was long enough for the man to lose him among the houses and shanties of the town.

And that's what he did, leaving the wagon road first and cutting through Nils Norgaard's pasture and entering Clantick between a log cabin and an abandoned sawmill, his tracks nearly disappearing in the short, brown grass. The cold ground being hard, the killer's mount left few marks in the sod, and Stillman finally gave up the calf. He knew that even if he took the time to trace the man's path through the back streets, he'd lose it eventually on a street where other horses had recently passed. The man was too smart to lead Stillman to his front door.

Stillman cursed loudly, wincing against the pain in his injured arm, and headed for Doc Evans's house on the hill.

Evans was playing checkers with the shell-shocked Civil War veteran, Hyram Pyle, when Stillman arrived. "Well, I'll be goddamned," Evans exclaimed, chewing a stogey as he inspected Stillman's arm. "More business." He got up from the kitchen table, kicked a chair against the wall, and said, "Sit. I'll get some water."

"Make it snappy, will you, Doc?" Stillman said, dropping heavily into the chair. "I have a meeting at one."

Evans filled an enamel basin from a wood bucket on the cupboard. "Ah, yes . . . I heard about that little fandango." He chuffed, then nodded at Stillman's bleeding arm. "What happened here?"

"We set a trap for the killer. It didn't work. He took a shot at me." Stillman winced and began removing his coat. "Crazy bastard." He noted that, from all appearances, the doctor had been sitting here for at least the past half hour, playing checkers with Hyram Pyle.

Stillman hadn't written anyone off his suspect list, which had included the whole town, but he thought he could safely write the doctor off, once and for all. And Hyram Pyle, who sat fidgeting across the table from Stillman, wincing and staring at the sheriff's bleeding arm, probably remembering similar disturbing sights at Stone's River and Pea Ridge.

Evans came over and helped Stillman with the coat. Then he cut the sleeve away from Stillman's arm, positioned the arm over the basin on the table, and dabbed cold water on the wound. Stillman winced and growled at the burning water, fidgeting in his seat. When the doctor had removed most of the blood, he adjusted his spectacles on his nose and scrutinized the two small holes, in the front and back of Stillman's left arm, just above the elbow.

His ironic eyes found Stillman's. "I bet that hurts like hell."

Stillman wagged his head. "You don't know the half of it, Doc. How fast can you sew it up? I gotta get a move on."

"Don't think it needs sewing, just wrapping."

Evans reached for a whiskey bottle. There was always a bottle of cheap whiskey on the doctor's table—that and a dozen books, scrawled notes, half a dozen dirty coffee cups and drink glasses, and an ashtray packed with cigar butts and ashes. He removed the cork with his teeth, spat it onto the table.

Tipping the bottle and pouring the searing liquid over the wound, he said, "This isn't going to make it feel any better, I'm afraid, but it'll keep the infection out."

The whiskey burned like a sharp knife cutting all the way to the bone, and Stillman's eyes watered from the pain. Ten minutes later, however, the wound was wrapped with gauze. Not exactly good as new—Evans ordered him to have the bandages changed twice daily for the next two weeks—but Stillman was ready to go.

The sheriff shrugged into his bloodstained coat.

"I'll see you there," Evans called to him as he made his way to the door, his arm feeling as though it had been bathed in hot tar.

Stillman turned. "You wanna watch me fry, do you, Doc?"

Evans squinted his eyes and poured himself and Hyram Pyle a drink from the bottle he'd just used to clean Stillman's arm. "I suspect you have something up your sleeve," he said. He turned to Pyle, who smiled witlessly down at his whiskey, like a child who'd just been bestowed with an unexpected gift. "And we wouldn't miss it for the world, would we, my good fellow?"

Stillman saw Fay, Leon, and Jody riding up the hill toward Evans's house as he started riding down on Dorothy. Leon and Fay were on Sweets.

"How's your arm?" Fay asked him.

"Good as new," he said with a smile.

"Like hell," she said.

"Well . . . almost." He turned to Leon. "They're having a little party for us over at the Boston."

McMannigle gave his head a slow wag. "Yeah . . . I kinda figured. Our week is up."

Stillman said, "Jody, will you take my darling wife over to the jail? Lock her up and keep an eye on her."

Jody slid his eyes from Stillman to Fay, then back
to Stillman. "Beg your pardon, Ben?"

"You heard me," Stillman said. "If she gives you
any trouble, use handcuffs." Stillman spurred Dorothy over to Fay. He kissed her quickly on the lips.
"Won't be for long."

She looked at him suspiciously. "What's on your
mind?"

"I think we've got the son of a bitch."

"Where?" she said, incredulous.

Leon's expression was similar to Fay's. "You
think he'll be at the *meeting?*"

Stillman nodded.

Fay said, "Why . . . ?"

"He thinks he's beaten us. He'll want to enjoy the
fruits of his labor."

"He'll just blend into the crowd, like he's always
done," Jody said darkly.

Stillman turned to the black-haired young man,
whose plainsman hat was secured to his head by a
horsehair strap and acorn fastener. "Yeah, but he'll
be the only one there with a bullet wound—outside
of me, that is."

"You hit him?" Leon asked.

"I think I creased his gizzard. Besides"—Stillman
smiled—"I think I know who it is."

"What?" they all exclaimed in unison.

Stillman removed a crumpled piece of paper from
his left sleeve. It was the note Doc Evans had seen
him swipe only a few minutes before, from Evans's

table. The doctor was far too good a cardsharp not to have seen Stillman's attempted sleight of hand.

Stillman held up the wind-ruffled scrap of paper and smiled a self-satisfied smile, his first smile of any kind in several days. "I have the killer's signature right here."

21

TWENTY MINUTES LATER, Stillman and McMannigle stood on the porch of the Boston Hotel, watching buggies and saddle horses converge on the hitchracks—mostly town council members and First Street businessmen. It was the first sign of life First Street had seen today, and everyone approached looking haggard and wary. After all, the killer was still on the loose and, as far as they knew, he'd strike at any one of them.

Only a few men glanced the lawmen's way as they headed past the hitchrack toward the steps, dour, indicting expressions etched on their features. Rolph Garrity and Edgar Tempe grimly helped Jeff Carney and his wheelchair up the steps. A minute after Jeff was safely in the building, seven soldiers in blue wool uniforms rode up on geldings sporting McClellan saddles.

One of the men Stillman recognized as Hoyt McAndrews, the major in charge of the garrison at

Fort Assiniboine. The man riding to his left was no doubt the second-in-command; he wore a captain's bars. McAndrews and the captain dismounted their horses, turned their reins over to two corporals, who remained mounted, and headed for the hotel.

Leon muttered dryly, "Looks like they've called in the cavalry."

"Can you blame them?" Stillman said. "Their town's under siege."

McMannigle only sighed and shook his head. He thought it insulting that the town council would unseat its sheriff because he couldn't stop a killer in only seven days. The older Stillman was more philosophical. He knew the council was only doing what it thought it had to do to save the town.

Six minutes after high noon, Garrity turned a sheepish gaze to Stillman and McMannigle. Then he turned and headed into the hotel.

"Well, I guess this is it," Stillman said with a sigh.

"I'll be here watching the doors," Leon said meaningfully. "Just holler if you need me."

When Stillman entered the dining room off the Boston's grand lobby, the room hushed, and all faces turned toward him. At the head of the room, the council members and Mayor Edgar Tempe sat along one side of a large, circular table, facing the twelve or so businessmen who'd gathered before them in Windsor chairs.

Stillman removed his hat and took a seat near the back of the room, not far from Mr. Auld, the liv-

eryman, who crossed his arms and worried a tooth-
pick between his lips. The only men not outfitted in
broadcloth suits were Auld and Jeff Carney, who sat
in his wheelchair in the center of the carpeted room,
about ten yards before the councilmen.

The other spectators—Frederick Miller, the gunsmith Julius Hallum, the mercantile owner Mr. Hall,
the newsman Evan Danielson, Doc Evans, and several others—sat at various white-clothed tables, hats
before them, legs crossed. The two soldiers sat up
near the councilmen, to the blacksmith's right.

An air of grim urgency hovered over the room,
which had been given over to the meeting, as it was
one night a month. A town hall had not yet been
constructed. Outside, dust and leaves blew against
the windows, and a splash of raindrops appeared on
the glass. Only the horses at the hitchrack moved
on the street.

Mayor Tempe sipped a glass of water and cleared
his throat. "Well, I guess we all know what we're
doing here."

He locked eyes with Stillman. "Ben, there's no
easy way to do this, so I'm just going to do it. We're
removing you and McMannigle." He indicated the
cavalry captain. "In light of the fact that one of his
own men was killed by this crazy man, Major
McAndrews has offered to fill the sheriff's office
and use his men to patrol the streets until we can
hire another lawman. Sorry, Ben, but something just
had to be done."

Stillman rose with a sigh. "I couldn't agree more, Mr. Mayor. No hard feelings. But the soldiers won't be necessary."

Rolph Garrity studied Stillman a moment, frowning, then said, "What are you talking about?"

"I know who the killer is."

Everyone in the room jerked their heads to Stillman. A roar went up. Garrity rose, lifted his hands, and yelled for quiet.

He studied Stillman again, unbelievingly. "Well?" he said, impatient. "Who?"

Stillman got up and walked toward the councilmen's table, holding his injured left arm stiffly at his side. He stopped behind Jeff Carney, who sat erect in his wheelchair, facing the councilmen at their circular table.

"Maybe Mr. Carney will tell us that."

The room was so silent you could hear air sluice through windpipes and the breeze push against the windows. All dubious faces were turned toward Stillman. They slid between him and Jeff Carney, who sat in his chair stiffly, not moving a muscle.

Stillman studied the back of the blacksmith's head. "How 'bout it, Jeff?" he prodded.

Carney turned his head around, a shocked, guilty expression flushing his big, deep-lined face, smoke and soot ingrained in every mark.

"What are you talkin' about, Ben?" His eyes stayed with Stillman for two heartbeats. Then he turned to the councilman, shrugging his shoulders and lifting his hands, befuddled. "I don't know what he's talkin' about."

"Give me a hand here, Jeff," Stillman said, his voice even. "Could it be"—in a blur of motion, he lifted his right leg and brought his foot hard against the back of the crippled man's chair—"*Dalton Bliss?*"

Stillman's voice boomed off the wainscoted walls and crystal chandeliers, making the whole room jump. Carney came out of the chair like a rock from a slingshot. Half-running, arms flailing wildly, he bolted headlong into the table where the councilmen sat behind their hats and water glasses.

Carney pushed off the table and turned toward Stillman. Simultaneously, he lowered his head and lifted his right arm, producing a long-bladed knife from a scabbard between his shoulderblades. Screaming, he heaved the knife end over end.

Stillman ducked. The blade whistled over his head and embedded itself in a table behind him, the bone handle quivering loudly. Having dropped to his knees to avoid the knife, Stillman lifted his head to see Carney wheel and run to his left, boots thundering across the carpet, past the two soldiers who sat dumbfounded, unable to move.

In half a second, Stillman's Colt was in his hand. He leveled his arm and loosed two quick rounds, the .44 spitting fire and smoke, just as Carney lowered his head, lifted his arms, and jumped through the window in a great, ear-numbing cacophony of shattering glass.

Stillman ran to the broken window and looked out. On the boardwalk below, Jeff Carney lay on his back, hands wrapped around his bloodied left knee, groaning and cursing and rolling from side to side in pain. Leon McMannigle stood over him, the deputy's rifle aimed at the man's pain-stricken face.

Leon lifted his eyes to Ben's. After a moment, he smiled with his eyes. Stillman heaved a sigh of relief. Turning to the men who'd congregated around him to look out the window, he made his way through the crowd, across the dining room, and outside. By the time he'd made it to the boardwalk, the others were on their way, as well.

"Oh, you bastard!" Carney roared at Stillman. "Oh, you goddamned murderin' bastard!"

Rolph Garrity ran up beside Stillman. His face epitomized pure confoundment. "What . . . ? What . . . ?" he cried, shaking his head and turning from Carney to Stillman.

The others gathered around, looking just as confounded as the chairman.

Stillman looked down at the writhing Carney. "Gentlemen, meet Dalton Bliss," he said. "His boys were hung here a few years back. He came to wreak havoc on the town."

"But . . . but . . . the *wheelchair*," Mayor Tempe said.

"All a put-on," Stillman replied. "His legs only

appear withered because his pants are so oversized, and because that's how you'd expect them to look. A cripple'd be the last person you'd expect guilty of murder. And indeed he was the last, until I learned from the sheriff over in Malta that the Bliss boys' father was a blacksmith and that his wife had hanged herself two days after the boys were lynched. Then, just this morning, I saw a note on Doc Evans's table."

Stillman plucked the paper from his pocket and handed it to Garrity.

" 'Who's gonna pay for this?' " Garrity read, and returned his puzzled eyes to Stillman.

Stillman found Doc Evans's face in the crowd and chuckled. "Apparently the doctor hasn't been payin' his smithy bills lately. But more important is the way our good blacksmith spelled who's. H-o-o-s-e. That's just how the killer spelled it on Leon's mirror. Not a dead giveaway—there's plenty of poor spellers in town, including myself—but that coupled with a few other things . . ." Stillman let his voice trail off as he knelt over the ailing Bliss. With one hand he ripped open the man's denim coat, then his shirt. A burlap rag, soaked with dark-red blood, was attached to his right side. "He's got a bullet in him that belongs to me. A few minutes ago I spotted fresh blood under his chair."

The men gathered around Stillman, McMannigle, and the writhing, cursing Dalton Bliss, were all just as perplexed as they'd been five minutes ago, and each said as much, all at once, demanding to know why such a harmless-seeming man as Jeff Carney would kill five innocent people. When Leon and Doc Evans had got the man into the doctor's wagon and had hauled him off to the jail, where the doctor would tend the man's wounds, Stillman turned to the murmuring crowd.

"What do you say we all go back into the hotel, and I'll explain it to you?"

Back in the dining room, with its broken window letting in the cool afternoon air, Stillman held court, the councilmen, army men, and townsmen gathered around. They listened carefully as Stillman, who lighted a cigar he bummed from Garrity, explained the botched stage holdup, the hanged boys, and the murdered witnesses at the Bliss boys' trial. He told about how Fay had been one of the witnesses, and about how, earlier in the day, she'd tried to lure the dead boys' grief-crazed father, Dalton Bliss, out from hiding.

"How were you so sure it was Bliss?" Edgar Tempe asked Stillman.

The sheriff shrugged and stared at the table grimly. "When I heard that his wife hanged herself two days after the boys were lynched, and that Bliss himself disappeared, never to be seen or heard from again—well, you put it together."

"That man must've been harboring a lot of hate, these five long years," Rolph Garrity said.

"I reckon he was biding his time," Stillman allowed. "I'm sure learning how to do smithy work in that wheelchair took a lot of practice."

"Why the hell you s'pose he went to all that work?" inquired Dwight Utley, the attorney on the town council.

Stillman took a long drag off the cigar. "I reckon he wanted very much to appear invisible which, as we all know, crippled people do. And he nearly was. He nearly got away with it. The only problem he ran into was himself. He might have started out acting on pure vengeance, but it looks to me like the hate twisted his mind, and he started to enjoy what he was doing. He started enjoying the cat-and-mouse game, and he started taking chances . . . like going after people in daylight . . . and bushwacking me."

Stillman pulled thoughtfully on the cigar as he tried to imagine how it would be: your sons hanged over a silly, albeit deadly stunt, your wife dead, everything you'd expected from life—your hopes and dreams—gone in the jerk of a hangman's knot. How quickly, easily we're driven to madness and murder. . . .

Ten minutes later, the meeting adjourned and Stillman walked down the hotel's steps to the street. He'd started toward the jailhouse when he saw Fay heading toward him. Apparently, she'd broke jail. Stillman smiled, watching her, her hair blowing in the wind, her face flushed from both the chill air and relief that the nightmare was finally over.

"Ben," someone called from the Boston's veranda.

Stillman turned to see Mayor Tempe, Rolph Garrity, and the other councilmen move toward him down the steps, the two army men following close behind.

Smiling contritely, pinching his mouth between thumb and index finger, the chairman said, "I and the rest of the town council, and Mayor Tempe here, just wanted to thank you . . . and . . ."

Stillman raised his good hand. "No apologies necessary. I know the position you men were in. Frankly, I probably would have done the same thing."

The mayor, councilmen, and soldiers studied the affable sheriff in silence, looking sheepish and cowed in spite of the lawman's reassurances.

Finally, Major McAndrews cleared his throat. "Well, I guess our services won't be needed after all." He tipped his hat once at the councilmen and once at Stillman, gave a nod, and headed for his horse. The captain did likewise. In a minute, they and their men were headed back toward the fort, and the mayor and councilmen silently, awkwardly dispersed.

At long last, Stillman found himself alone with his lovely wife, with no killer at large. Fay slid up against him, touched her gloved hand to his big cheek, and kissed his lips.

Stillman stared deep into her smoky brown eyes. "So you sprung yourself, eh?"

"Scot-free," Fay said. She turned back toward the jail, a melancholy look clouding her face. "You know, seeing him in there. . . Mr. Bliss. . . " She shook her head, unable to find the words to express her haunted thoughts.

"Part of you feels sorry for him, doesn't it?" Stillman said.

"Yes . . . yes, it does."

They stared thoughtfully at the jailhouse for several seconds. Then Stillman turned to Fay, taking her arm. "Come on. Let's go home for a while."

She turned to him again, and smiled. "Let's."

Stillman untethered Dorothy's reins from the hitchrack. Arm in arm, he and Fay led the horse toward French Street and home.

EPILOGUE

AFTER SCHOOL FOUR days later, when all the other children had gone home, Candace Hawley stayed behind to clean the chalkboards while Fay tried to catch up on her grading before she and Candace met Ben and Mrs. Hawley over at the Boston later for supper.

Candace and her mother, Noreen, had returned to town after the killer had been caught, making it easier for Candace to attend school with Fay. They were staying once again with Fay and Ben, who'd taken the little girl horseback riding every afternoon for the past three days. Ben seemed to have enjoyed the outings as much as Candace. It had given him a chance to relax after his seemingly interminable ordeal with the killer. A child's innocence can be deeply affecting, not to mention soothing. That was one of the things Fay enjoyed most about her job.

Fay was grading Tommy Kyle's algebra quiz

when Candace suddenly turned away from the chalkboards.

"Mrs. Stillman?" she asked.

Fay lifted her pen and turned to the girl, smiling at how assertive and talkative the child had gradually become. "Yes, Candace?"

"Do you think it's possible that I could be a poetess someday like Miss Dickinson?"

Fay set her pen down and turned her whole body to the child, giving Candace her full attention. "Why, Candace! Do you like Emily Dickinson?"

Shyly, the girl turned back to the blackboard, moving her damp cloth slowly across the slate. She shrugged. "Well, just what I read in our English reader."

"That's wonderful. All the other students have been complaining about how hard she is."

Candace shrugged again. Her cheeks colored proudly. "I especially liked the poem that compares ships to books. Even memorized it."

Fay was flabbergasted. "Candace, you didn't!"

Candace jerked one shoulder again, as though it was no big deal, and mumbled, "Sure."

Fay grabbed her arm and turned the child around. "Let's hear."

Grinning from ear to ear, the little dark-haired girl folded her hands before her, took a deep breath, raised up and down on the balls of her feet, and recited very proudly and precisely:

*"There is no Frigate like a Book
To take us Lands away
Nor any Coursers like a Page
Of prancing Poetry—*

*This Traverse may the poorest take
Without oppress of Toll—
How frugal is the Chariot
That bears the Human Soul!"*

Fay stared at the lovely girl for several seconds, her eyes filming with tears. She slapped a hand to her chest and swallowed hard to keep from crying aloud and making a total fool of herself. Her heart felt swollen as large as a harvest moon.

"Oh, Candace," she cried at last, finding her voice, flicking a tear from her cheek and steepling her hands beneath her chin. "That was beautiful, truly beautiful."

The girl shrugged again and looked down at the new gingham dress Fay and Mrs. Hawley had sewn for her. "I'm not sure what it all means, but after lookin' up some of the harder words in the dictionary, I think it means something like how books can take us as far away as some ships—that's a frigate, I guess. And I think it sorta also means that, since books are cheap, even those of us without much money can afford to travel." Both tiny shoulders rose and fell again in an offhand shrug.

Fay shook her head and beamed at the girl. "Can-

dace, you're a brilliant child! You're going to be a
thrilling poet."

"You think?" Candace asked. "As good as Miss
Dickinson?"

"Well, those are some mighty big shoes to fill,
but I think if ever there was one to fill them, it's
you, Miss Hawley."

There was a knock at the door. Fay stood, swept
the hair back from Candace's face with a loving
hand, and made her way to the door at the front of
the schoolroom. Opening it, she was surprised to see
Noreen Hawley, in a heavy coat and with a crisp
wool scarf on her head. Her face was painted, and
her eyes were happier than Fay had ever seen them.
Since Candace had been walking home after school
with Fay, Fay hadn't expected to see Noreen here.

Fay saw that a green wagon waited on the road
beyond the picket fence encircling the schoolyard.
A closer look told her that the man driving was Earl
Hawley, all dressed up in a Sunday suit and derby
hat, his barbered hair slicked back behind his ears.
His face was clean-shaven, and he looked at Fay
directly, even giving his head a small nod in greeting.

Fay turned her eyes back to Noreen, who smiled
demurely before her. Before Fay could say anything,
Mrs. Hawley said, "He came to your house to pick
me up earlier. I wasn't sure if I should go, but he
looked so nice." Noreen bobbed her head as she
laughed, tossing a look at Earl behind her. Swinging

her head back to Fay, she said, "He took me over
to the café and bought me lunch, and we talked it
all out. I think he's done drinkin' now. That's what
he says, and"—she looked at her hands—"and . . .
well, I believe him."

Fay clutched the woman's hands in hers. "Noreen,
are you sure?"

"I guess as sure as I can be," Mrs. Hawley said.
"He's promised me, and I told him that if he ever
gets . . . you know . . . that way again, I'll take Candace away for good." She'd been speaking to her
shoes, and she lifted her eyes now to Fay's. "And I
will."

Fay studied her, then she smiled and nodded.
"Okay."

She turned and called for Candace, who came
running. "Momma?"

"You're going home, child," Fay said. "Get your
coat."

Candace studied her mother skeptically. "Is . . . is
everything . . . ?"

"Everything's going to be just fine, my girl," Mrs.
Hawley said, touching her hand to the child's face.
"I promise you that."

Candace stood there for several seconds, sliding
her eyes between her mother and her father, sitting
on the green wagon out on the road. "I'll get my
coat," she said and ran to the cloakroom.

Fay watched the girl go, then turned to Mrs. Hawley. "Noreen," she said, "I hope this means that Can-

dace will be able to attend school regularly."

"He promised that, too, Mrs. Stillman. And I'll see to it. Don't you worry." Noreen Hawley gazed directly into Fay's eyes. "I can't tell you how much you helped me . . . you and your husband . . . seein' how you live." She gave a nervous laugh. "I guess a woman needs to stick up for herself at times."

Fay smiled. "Good luck, Noreen."

"Thanks again, Mrs.—"

"Fay, Noreen. Please."

The woman smiled. "Fay."

Fay turned to see Candace standing beside them, dressed in her wool coat, knit cap, and mittens. She clutched her reader to her breast.

"Wait just a minute," Fay said. She walked to her desk and came back with a book, which she gave to Candace. "This is for you," she told the girl. "They're poems by Miss Dickinson. I give them to you with the stipulation that you take it with you on long walks in the hills this spring, and enjoy them at your leisure."

Candace's eyes were large as saucers as she riffled through the small, leather-bound volume in her mittened hands. "Wow! A whole book of Miss Dickinson's poems. Look, Ma! Thank you, Mrs. Stillman."

Fay bent down and rested her hands on the child's shoulders. "Remember this, Candace. It's Miss Dickinson again:

"We never know how high we are
Till we are called to rise
And then, if we are true to plan
Our statures touch the skies."

Candace smiled brightly.

"Thank you again, Fay," Noreen said. "Thanks for everything."

As they headed down the path to the gate, the brittle wind whipping their clothes, Candace turned and said, "Please say good-bye to Mr. Stillman for me."

"Oh, I will, Candace," Fay returned. "I will . . . and see you tomorrow . . . bright and early."

Fay stood in the open door, braving the cold to watch Noreen and Candace Hawley mount the green wagon. When they were all situated and ready to go, Earl turned toward Fay. For a moment, Fay felt her stomach turn. But then the man lifted his hat from his head, smiled, gave a nod, donned the hat, and slapped the reins against the horse's back.

Candace and Mrs. Hawley waved as the wagon turned into the street. Fay waved back, fighting tears. When the wagon was out of sight, she stepped into the building, shivering but buoyant, and closed the door behind her.

No one knows the American West better.

JACK BALLAS

❏ *THE HARD LAND*

0-425-15519-6/$5.99

❏ *BANDIDO CABALLERO*

0-425-15956-6/$5.99

❏ *GRANGER'S CLAIM*

0-425-16453-5/$5.99

The Old West in all its raw glory.